A Well-Timed Enchantment

A WELL-TIMED ENCHANTMENT

Vivian Vande Velde

Crown Publishers, Inc. · New York

To Elizabeth (even if you don't like the ending)—
May all your wishes come true.

Published by Crown Publishers, Inc., a Random House Company, 225 Park Avenue South, New York, New York 10003
CROWN is a trademark of Crown Publishers, Inc.
Manufactured in the United States of America

Library of Congress Cataloging-in-Publication Data
Velde, Vivian Vande.
A well-timed enchantment / Vivian Vande Velde.
p. cm.
Summary: A girl and her cat disappear back in time to retrieve a lost watch.
ISBN 0-517-57319-9
0-517-57340-7 (lib. bdg.)
[1. Time travel—Fiction. 2. Cats—Fiction] I. Title.
PZ7.V489WE 1990 [Fic]—dc20 89-22225

10 9 8 7 6 5 4 3 2 1

First Edition

Contents

1 / Deanna

Summer in France was a once-in-a-lifetime opportunity for a fifteen-year-old girl, a social and cultural experience she'd never forget.

At least, that's what everyone told Deanna.

"Travel broadens," they'd said. "Unique perspective," they'd said. Etc., etc., etc. Nobody thought to ask her if she wanted to go.

"I don't understand French," she'd complained, speaking in a little voice, as she and her mother packed.

Her mother had laughed. "You'll pick it up. And I'll be there to help you. And don't forget, more French people speak English than American people speak French. Don't worry about it." Easy for her to say. Besides French and English, Deanna's mother spoke Italian and Russian, could get by in Spanish and German, had a smattering of Dutch, and knew how to say "Please" and "Thank you" and "Is this water fit to drink?" in Hungarian. She'd never had to sit in a roomful of strangers, all chattering away incomprehensibly, hour after hour after hour.

2

Deanna kept her head down as she walked. If she didn't see the Guyon farmhouse, she could pretend she was back home, crossing an American field, on her way to visit her friends.

These French people were her maternal relatives: aunts and uncles and cousins her mother hadn't seen in years, people Deanna had never seen. They'd give her big kisses, one on each cheek, and smile at her. *"Ne parle t-elle pas français?"* they'd ask, which Deanna learned meant "Doesn't she speak French?" And her mother would rattle off an explanation of how Deanna had spoken a little when she'd been very young but had forgotten it all.

Sometimes she'd hear her father's name mentioned, or they'd say *"ton mari"*—your husband—and since Deanna knew they were talking about the divorce, she could almost follow what was being said. But then they'd be off onto something else, and Deanna was just sitting there, looking at the flowered wallpaper, wishing she were back home.

It wasn't fair.

Deanna scuffed her sneakers along the dirt path that ran from the Guyon farm to the cottage of their neighbor, Madame LeBrun.

Summer in France. It wasn't as though they were sunbathing on the Riviera, or touring the Louvre in Paris, or exploring the castles in the Loire Valley. Chalon was farm country. Grapes and cheese and the occasional cow. A once-in-a-lifetime opportunity. Sure. Unless you've been to Wisconsin or Iowa.

Deanna turned around and put her hands on her

hips. "Are you coming, Oliver, or not? Because I'm not chasing you through all those weeds again."

The small cat sat down on the path. As though to prove who was in charge, he began a meticulous grooming of his thick black fur.

"Right. That's it." Deanna whirled around and continued walking. Let him catch up if he wanted to. Or not. It made no difference to her. It was bad enough she was reduced to talking to a cat, she wasn't going to argue with him. Especially since he was a French cat and probably didn't understand any more English than Madame LeBrun's daughter.

She stopped where the path widened at the old stone well and sat on the edge. She twirled her ponytail around her finger, trying to tuck the hair—which she liked to think of as dark blond but which everybody else persisted in calling light brown—into a bun. As always, it fell loose again immediately. She was supposed to have helped Madame LeBrun bake a pie today, something to which she had been looking forward since it had been decided last Thursday. (*Jeudi:* The days of the week were one thing Deanna knew, though she had to start at Monday and work her way through in order. She could also count from one to twenty if you weren't fussy about fourteen and fifteen.)

Madame LeBrun was a friendly old woman, one of those French people who knew more English . . . and so forth. But she hadn't been well today. Her daughter, who spoke no English, had been able to get that much across to Deanna. Back home in Greeley, Colorado, there'd be pool parties and movies and roller-skating, a last rush of activities before school started, and here she was downcast and with nothing to do because she hadn't gotten to help bake an apple pie.

Oliver had followed after all and jumped up onto the well, then into her lap. Absently Deanna stroked his thick fur. He had become a steady companion ever since she'd rescued him from the neighbors' dog last month. Her one friend. *Now that's a bit overdone,* she chided herself. *Sentimental is one thing, but let's not get downright melodramatic.*

She ran a finger along the worn stone. "How old's this well, I wonder," she said out loud. The farmhouse had running water, and the well had obviously not been used in ages: there was no bucket and some of the stones were crumbling. Back home, in Greeley, people would have torn the whole thing down, or at least put up a sign warning that it was unsafe. But there were a lot of unimaginably old things in France.

Oliver, uninterested, looked at her with his big green eyes and rubbed his head against her hand to get her attention back to petting.

"Pretty old, I'd say." Deanna peered down the well. The hole was too dark or too deep for her to see water. It smelled like water though. It looked like a model for the kind of well cartoon characters would make wishes into. "Hello." Her voice bounced off the mossy stones and came back to her in a faint singsong echo. "Anybody home? *Est-ce que . . . Est-ce qu'il y a . . .*" She couldn't manage it in French and instead dug a coin, an old copper *centime,* out of her pocket. She tossed it into the well. Several seconds later she heard the soft plunk as it hit water. It echoed, almost musically.

Oliver became suddenly restive.

"What's the matter, afraid of getting wet?" Deanna asked, trying to settle him back into her lap. She gazed into the well. "I wish . . . " She hesitated, thinking. "I wish . . . " She wished too many things and shrugged.

The cat arched his back, his fur on end, and hissed.

He squirmed out from under her hands, scratching her to get away. He stood on the stone edge of the well, stiff-legged and tense, staring down into the darkness.

"Miserable thing," she muttered. On top of everything else, trying to manage him she'd caught her wristwatch on her sweater. Just above the leather band a trickle of blood appeared—a series of tiny red bumps along where the cat had scratched her. She hurried to unfasten the clasp before she bled on the sweater.

Oliver gave a particularly loud hiss and Deanna jumped. The loosened watch slid from around her wrist and dropped into the well. "Oh, no." She heard it hit the water. Her father had bought that watch for her at Disneyland last year, just about the last time she could remember the family being together and happy. Or, at least, before she realized they were unhappy. "Now look what you've made me do."

Oliver had leapt off the well and was standing on the grass, his fur all on end.

"What is the matter with you?" Deanna turned away from him when she heard a gurgling from the well. Now, strangely, she saw the glint of water, where before there had been none to see.

Meanwhile, Oliver was hissing and spitting, carrying on the same as he had when he'd been stuck in the tree, the neighbors' dog trying to make lunch out of him.

Deanna had no more than glanced at him, but when she looked back at the well, the water had risen high enough to see clearly. For a moment she had the awful thought that it was her fault, that she had somehow broken the well, plugged it by dropping her watch. But that was ridiculous.

And what was that sound? That strange hint of music in the air?

No.

That hint of music in the water. The water that was now high enough to touch.

Cautiously, Deanna eased herself off the well. The water rose, almost to the edge now, and glimmered despite the overcast sky. Beside her, Oliver arched his back and spat. "Come on, Oliver," she said unsteadily, backing away.

A hand reached out of the well and grabbed Deanna's arm.

She gave one startled cry, then lost her balance. The sky tipped. The cold water closed over her head. She struggled against the hands that dragged her down, down, down. The walls of the well sped past. She twisted frantically, but all that accomplished was to get herself facing backward, so that she couldn't even see who held her but could only see where she had been. Even if she got loose, could she ever reach the surface before her aching lungs forced her to take a fatal breath? The patch of sky receded, narrowed. Far above she saw Oliver, pacing the edge of the well opening, but her ears were filled with the rush of water and the sound of someone, somewhere below her, singing.

The last thing she was aware of was Oliver leaping in after her.

2 / The Well

Deanna could smell the sweet grass that cushioned her cheek. The warmth of the sun had just about dried the clothes on her back, though her front was still damp and prickly. Birds chattered and insects buzzed and chittered.

Obviously someone had rescued her. Someone had seen her lose her balance and fall in the well—Deanna dismissed the reaching hand as part of her momentary dizziness—someone had seen her fall, and had pulled her out.

Deanna opened her eyes. A thick wall of trees bordered the glade in which she lay. She raised her head. More trees, tall and mossy. A pond to her left. It was edged on its farther side by willows trailing into the still water. Beyond that, the woods resumed. Not a sign of the well, or fields, or cows.

Obviously someone had pulled her out of the well, carried her miles away from the Guyon farm, and found a forest clearing to let her revive in.

Sure.

She raised herself up onto her elbows.

Oliver sat nearby, fastidiously washing his face with his paws, ignoring her. More trees formed a backdrop behind him.

"Bonjour," said a voice from behind her, from where she had already looked and seen no one. *"Bienvenue."*

Deanna craned around, fast enough to put a crick in her neck. But that didn't give her a clear view, so she rolled over onto her back, then sat up. There.

Sitting didn't help. The speaker had a long, flowing gown of some material that seemed to mix silk and silver, a sword, and shoulder-length hair of fluorescent chartreuse.

"Bonjour," the man repeated, this time louder and more distinctly. For a moment she just stared. Then she closed her eyes and hoped he'd go away.

"Bienvenue." He pronounced each syllable as though she might be hard-of-hearing and reading his lips.

"Bonjour," she whispered, never opening her eyes. Hello couldn't hurt.

He rattled off something else that went on and on. A second voice chimed in and Deanna looked in spite of herself. Another man had come out of nowhere to join the first. Tall, slender, young, heartbreakingly beautiful—which, actually, described both of them—this one was dressed in two-tone jeans and a black *Rock 'n' Roll Forever* T-shirt. He wore a sword, too, and although his hair had less green in it, it still had that glow-in-the-dark quality that made Deanna's head hurt. Who were they? Where was she? And most important of all, what in the world was going on?

The strange men stopped whatever it had been that they were saying and looked at each other as though to say, *Oh, no, not again.* "*Bonjour,*" the first repeated in his infuriatingly slow, over-enunciated way. "*Bienvenue.*" As in *Let's start at the beginning again.*

"Look," Deanna said. "I don't speak French, so you might as well stop talking like I'm an idiot. Because no matter how slow and careful you talk, I can't understand you." She folded her arms defiantly. It hadn't been fair of her mother to drag her to France unprepared: *You'll pick it up,* indeed! Her mother accused her of not even trying, but what about the others? French people pronounced Deanna *Dionne* and smiled condescendingly when she corrected them as though she was the one who didn't know any better. Until they got it right, she wasn't giving an inch.

The men conferred in soft voices. Not French, she realized a moment before they stopped, something with different rhythms and cadences altogether.

"You're American," the one with the chartreuse hair said.

Deanna nodded eagerly "Y—"

"Twentieth century, I'd guess."

Her relief at hearing his accentless English evaporated.

"Nineteen-seventies or eighties," the other agreed. "Possibly nineteen-nineties: I lose track of time."

Deanna glanced at him apprehensively and was surprised to see that she had been mistaken about his shirt. Actually it was navy blue instead of black, which was a natural enough mistake, and instead of *Rock 'n' Roll Forever* it had the *No Smoking* symbol, which was not a natural mistake at all. "Who are you?" she asked. She hated the way her voice shook. This was worse than Sunday dinner with the entire Guyon family.

"Ah!" the one with the chartreuse hair said, pointing a finger at her. "Ah! Exactly! That is exactly not the question! The question is who are *you*?"

"My na—"

"And what," the second man cut in, "do you mean by going around throwing garbage into temporal loopholes?"

"I don't even—"

"Mucking up the astral planes," the first said.

"Destroying entire worlds without a backward glance." That was the second again.

Deanna had been taught that it was impolite to interrupt, but knew that was a rule adults rarely applied to themselves. She sat with her arms folded and waited for them to finish.

"Warping the fabric of time." The second man's shirt had changed once more. It was now purple, and bore the words: *¿Que Pasa?* "High-tech in a no-tech continuum," he said. "Didn't you stop to think? Didn't you care?"

They petered off when it became obvious she wasn't going to try to answer, and the chartreuse-haired one prompted, "Well?"

"I have no idea," Deanna said, "what you're talking about."

"Idiot human," the other muttered, turning his back to her, just soft enough that Deanna couldn't be sure if she was supposed to hear or not.

"Your timepiece: your miserable, high-tech, world-altering, digital timepiece that you flung into the temporal loophole."

Deanna looked from one to the other. "My Mickey Mouse watch?" she asked. "That fell into the well?"

"Exactly."

Deanna was willing to believe she'd done something awful because she was always accidentally breaking or spilling things. Her mother would smile knowingly and call it "that awkward stage." It seemed as though she had been at "that awkward stage" half her life. But she couldn't see what her lost watch had to do with anything. "What about it?"

"What about it? What about it? Time twists, nature shudders, civilization as we know it crumbles and she asks WHAT ABOUT IT?"

"I have no idea," Deanna repeated, more loudly and less patiently, "what you are talking about."

The yellow-haired one sighed loudly. He still kept his back to her, letting his companion do the talking.

"The temporal loophole—"

"The well," Deanna interrupted, determined to keep the conversation at as normal a level as she could.

"You opened the gateway." Then, when she looked at him blankly, "Between the physical and the metaphysical worlds." He sighed grandly and rolled his eyes. "You wished."

The man with the green *Kiss-Me-I'm-Irish* T-shirt

whirled around. "Or rather, you declared your intention to wish. And then—with the portals of sorcery open, with the powers of thaumaturgy invoked, attentive, and poised, with enchantment in the air, with incantations waiting to be completed—you . . . you . . . YOU . . . dropped . . . your . . . watch."

"I'm sorry," said Deanna. "Did it hurt something?"

"Argh!" The man pulled his glowing hair and turned his back to her again.

"I didn't know it was really a magic well."

"Well, no," the chartreuse-haired man simpered. "Of course you didn't. It wasn't like it was obvious or anything."

"It wasn't." Deanna was beginning to get annoyed with these two and their know-everything attitude.

"Of course it was obvious. Even your cat could see it. Don't tell me you're admitting your cat's smarter than you are?"

The man in the T-shirt nodded.

Deanna pretended not to notice. She glanced at Oliver, who was a bristling huddle, watching the two strangers apprehensively. She remembered how peculiar he'd been acting by the well and shivered. "Where did the watch go?" she asked.

"Back in time. To the dawning of the technological world." He must have seen her blank look. "Just north of 1066."

"Just north . . . ?" She decided not to ask. She had the feeling her next question was probably too obvious already. "So what?"

The first man sighed, loudly. "So here's humankind, poised on the brink of striking out on its own, putting its trust in logic, just beginning—just at the very beginning of turning its collective back on magic—when: wham!" He slammed his fist into his palm, making Deanna jump. "Something beyond all logic: an artifact, a talisman, a message from the supernatural; to wit: Here is magic; it exists, it's stronger than your nebulous science, put your trust here."

Deanna gulped. "My Mickey Mouse watch?"

"Now you've got it: You've just gone and changed history, kiddo."

"I *am* sorry," she said. "What exactly does the watch do?"

The man rolled his eyes again. "What does it do? *What does it do*?" He counted out on his fingers. One: "Some people will think it's a message from God—proof of an afterlife; others will be sure it's a gift from Satan. That means suicides both ways." He put out a second finger. "It falls into the hands of the religious leaders of the day. Debating the watch's significance, the medieval Church will divide against itself four hundred years too early. This means good-bye to the feudal system it should have fostered." A third finger. "With no central authority, everybody wants that watch. Even those who don't want it want it—can't let it fall into the other guy's hands, don't you see? That means wars." He tapped his fourth finger. "In the collapse of dynasties, key people don't get born. Result? No Renaissance to speak of. No Renaissance: no Age of Exploration. No Age of Exploration: no discovery of America." He'd run out of fingers on that hand and waved both hands in the air. "Not to mention the bubonic plague and how that'll last ten years longer than it should because nobody wants to risk harming the creature whose image appears on *your* watch."

Deanna gulped. "I *am* sorry," she repeated. She looked the two men over. (One with chartreuse hair, one with a pink T-shirt proclaiming *Suzuki Violin.*) "So who are you? Some kind of guardians of time?"

The one with the T-shirt rolled his eyes. "Is that what you think we look like?"

She didn't think he really wanted to hear what she thought they looked like and paused to consider. She concentrated on their beautiful, almost ethereal faces, on the one's fickle T-shirt and the other's gown which shimmered with otherworldly colors. "Elves," she said, before she was even aware of the word forming in her mind.

The first winced. *"Elves* has such ridiculous connotations—don't you think?—helping shoemakers and such."

"Though it is better," the second observed, "than some of what we've been called."

His friend ignored him. "We prefer Sidhe, even though that's Gaelic instead of Gallic, or fair folk."

"This whole thing is ridiculous," Deanna said. Where were her parents when she needed them? "This is absolutely ridiculous."

"Yes, isn't it? So we're sending you to fix the mess

you've made, to retrieve your watch. To make things the way they were before."

Of course she wanted the watch back in any case; it was *her* watch, given to her by *her* father. But surely there was someone better suited. She said, "Look. If there were . . . If you are—" She felt silly saying it. "—'fair folk,' then you yourselves are magic. You can fix things back to the way they're supposed to be."

"I told you she was dumber than the cat," muttered the T-shirted one.

"No," the other explained to her. "It's your world that is going to change, not ours. Besides, we don't have that much magic left. Magic has been disappearing for centuries, gradually, easily, gracefully. We've learned to make do with just a little. Sure, eventually we could right things. If we had the inclination and you had the time. But you have one day. Then things will start to change. History will begin to reshape itself. Do you understand? Twenty-four hours, and then nobody will even remember that the past used to be different. And you—you, little girl—won't even exist in that world. So you better do something about it quick."

"But how? I mean, even if I was willing—"

"Find the watch. Go back in time. Brave untold dangers. Destroy evil. Defend justice. *Find the watch.*"

This talk of destroying and defending was making Deanna nervous. "Where? I don't even know where to begin."

"Well, right here is a good place to start. We're in

medieval France. What *is* this? Do we have to tell you *every*thing? If it was easy, ducky, we wouldn't need you to do it."

The other, his red-and-white shirt bearing the message *COKE*, leaned closer to his companion and repeated, "I told you she was dumber than the cat."

"The cat?" the first echoed. "Do you think we should send the cat to help her?"

The other shrugged.

"Now wait a minute," Deanna said. "You're not sending anyone. I'm not going." She wasn't even sure she believed all this, and anyway she was expected back for lunch.

"Fine. Just be aware that you can't get home from here. Time here travels at a different rate." Then, to the other: "What good would a cat be?"

The more normal-looking one said, "It doesn't have to *be* a cat."

"Would you listen to me?" Deanna said. "I'm sure you could find someone who'd be much better at—"

The first fair folk glanced appraisingly at Oliver, who arched his back and made a sound very like a growl. "Good thought. If nothing else, the cat can listen to her complain." He waved his hand. The air sparkled and snapped.

"Oh my gosh," Deanna whispered.

"Not bad," the T-shirted one said.

"Try not to mess things up too badly," the one with the chartreuse hair told her. "And remember: you have twenty-four hours."

Both began to shimmer, to fade. Deanna could see

through them, to the trees behind them. Faintly she heard one ask the other, "So, who are you taking to the dance tonight?" The last thing she saw before they dissolved into nothingness was a lavender shirt with the words *Auf Wiedersehen*.

Then she turned to Oliver.

3 / Oliver

Whatever Oliver was, he definitely wasn't a cat any longer.

What he looked like was a young man—a boy—a year or two older than Deanna. He had dropped to a crouch and was watching her at least as apprehensively as she was watching him. He was dark-haired but pale-skinned, his eyes the same shade of green as they had been . . . before. Black rough-spun pants and shirt, vest of black fur (not, presumably, from a cat), a sword similar to the ones the fair folk had worn: his appearance was indeed vaguely . . . medieval.

Deanna found herself dressed in a lilac-colored gown with matching slippers and hat. The hat, she thought, after examining it, looked like a dunce cap with attached scarf.

Oliver inched backward, as though afraid of her. Deanna remembered how he had leapt into the water after her, going against his nature to rescue her and she hated that something about her made him afraid. "It's all right," she reassured him, though she felt it was unfair that there was no one around to reassure *her*. "We're still friends. Don't run away; we'll never find each other again if you run away."

He hesitated, his large green eyes never leaving her face.

Deanna stepped forward, but stopped when Oliver looked ready to bolt. She fought the inclination to say, "Come here, Oliver, come on, boy." She was vaguely uneasy, looking at Oliver the timid but attractive youth, as she remembered Oliver the cat, who would put his head in her lap and listen—or at least not interrupt—while she talked of how she missed home, missed the way things used to be. She began to get angry, not at him, but at the two fair folk. They hadn't asked his permission to turn him into a human any more than they had asked her if she wanted to come here and go on this ridiculous quest. Just because it was the human and not the elfin community in danger. . . .

She became aware of Oliver watching her, all the while watching her. Never moving, never blinking. Cat-like, she thought, before she realized what she'd thought. She wondered how much he could read from her face.

"Don't run away," she repeated, for that was what she feared the most.

Oliver stayed where he was, but that may have been because she had stayed where she was.

"Do you understand English?" she asked.

He nodded, slowly.

Impatiently, for she had been through a lot for a summer morning, she snapped, "Do you *speak* English?"

He blinked. He might have given the faintest hint of a smile, she couldn't be sure. "I do now." The voice was as thoroughly human as the face.

Now what? With a sigh, Deanna sat down on the ground. "Well," she said. "Any ideas?"

Again a blink. "About what, specifically?"

Deanna chose the most pressing question. "About where to find my time-traveling watch?"

Oliver glanced around the glade. "It's probably not here."

"No," she agreed, unsure whether Oliver was slow-witted or just had a weird sense of humor. "Probably not." He was supposed to *help* her. Maybe he was waiting for her to make the decisions. She wasn't used to making decisions. She was used to crossing her fingers and hoping for the best. She stood. "But where do we start? How do we get out of here?"

Oliver got to his feet, a graceful uncurling motion. "We could try the path."

There was no path: Deanna had seen that when she'd first glanced around the glade. But she humored Oliver; she looked where he was looking. She saw a road, paved with red polka-dot linoleum and marked with a flashing road-construction arrow.

"Good thought," she said.

This time she was sure he smiled. She found it oddly reassuring. She stepped onto the red-and-white linoleum and forced her voice into more brightness than she felt. "Wishing well," she said. "Elves. Next thing you know, we'll be meeting a frog demanding kisses."

"What—" He fell into step next to her. "—frog?"

"You know: a talking frog. Under a spell by an evil wizard? Kiss him and he turns back into a prince?"

"Kiss him?"

She glanced at his blank face. "Like in fairy tales."

"Fairy tales," he repeated, as blankly as he had repeated *Kiss him*.

If he had been one of those toy robots with the clear heads, she would have seen the wheels and gears going around for sure. Her assurance melted away, leaving her cold and empty. "Fairy tales," she said. "You read them to amuse yourself." She forced her voice to be stronger. "They're stories. A story's a kind of a . . . sort of made up . . . uhm. . . ."

He watched her steadily as she faltered, her hands waving vaguely. Then, when she gave up, he said, "I understand the words *fairy tale* and *story*."

She found his eyes oddly unsettling. The pupils were round like a human's, not slitted like a cat's, but he stood too close and stared at her too directly.

"Most likely, there won't be any story characters here."

"No, I just meant . . . Never mind." She pretended to be engrossed in their surroundings—the road, the trees, the occasional flashing arrow. Anything but Oliver. She was aware of him still looking at her. Great. Here she'd spent two minutes with a cat turned human, and already he thought she was an idiot. What do you say to a cat who can answer back? Deanna said nothing.

4 / The Clearing

What to say? Where to start? Deanna wanted to thank Oliver for jumping in the well after her, but didn't know how. Did he remember he was really a cat? (And if he didn't, should she tell him?) What did it feel like to change? Had it been painful? Did he regret it? Did he know any more about where they were and what they were supposed to be doing than she did?

Words had never come easy to Deanna. She had frequently found herself unexpectedly, unintentionally, in the background, even among her friends. And now, after a summer spent with distant relatives who spoke little if any English, she found it even harder than normal to get started. *Thank you, Oliver,* she'd say. *Thank you?* she could imagine him saying. Or, he'd ask *For what?* Or, if she worked out an answer for either of those, he'd say something else for which she didn't have an answer. Then she'd go and trip over her own tongue again, and Oliver would look at her with those big green eyes again, watching her make a fool of herself. Again.

So, instead of working out what to say to Oliver, her mind returned to the two fair folk and what they'd said about the well. It *had* been magic. If she'd made a wish, her wish would have come true. This is what she got for not being ready. She would never let it happen again. If she ever got a second shot at wishing, words would not be her downfall. *I wish that Mom and Dad were back together again,* that's what she'd wish. But though she'd never believed in magic until fifteen minutes ago, she'd heard about wishing and how tricky that could be, so she'd say: *I wish that Mom and Dad were back together again and that we'd all be happy again, forever and ever.* That's what she'd wish for them, whether they wanted it or not. But she probably never would get a second shot at wishing. She probably wouldn't even exist tomorrow.

Oliver put his hand on her arm, holding her back.

"What—?" she started, but he put his finger to his lips.

She looked around, saw nothing. Listened, heard nothing. She shook her head, but Oliver wasn't looking at her. He was continuing forward, but carefully, silently. *Stalking,* she thought.

For the first time Deanna realized that while she had been absorbed in her thoughts, the linoleum had ended, leaving only a path through the forest. And, now that she thought about it, there had been no flashing arrows for quite a while. She looked behind. No sign of red polka dots. In fact, the path seemed narrower back there, and overgrown, which she hadn't noticed as they'd walked. She checked forward to see the condition of the path where they had to go. Wide and clear as far as she could see—which, with the ups and downs and weaving between trees, admittedly wasn't far.

Oliver was developing quite a lead despite the fact that he was obviously taking care to move quietly.

She took one final glance backward. The path had faded in the last couple of seconds, narrower yet, and—not twenty feet from her—a large tree had sprouted. Its gnarled roots and the cherry blossoms that had fallen from its branches obliterated much of the path where they had just passed. Cherry blossoms in August? Even as she watched, the cherries formed, then ripened, then browned and withered and dropped to the ground.

She ran to catch up to Oliver. He stopped immediately, with a scowl for all her noise. She grabbed his arm. "Did you see—"

This time he laid his finger against her lips. Now she could hear it too: voices, coming from up ahead. "Someone to help us?" she guessed. "Since the fair folk led us here?"

Oliver gave her that look again—the one that indicated she was an idiot but he was too polite to say so.

She walked beside him, wondering how her slippered feet could make more noise than his boots.

The trees thinned. She could hear the voices more clearly. A horse whinnied. Harnesses jangled. Deanna and Oliver stopped short at the edge of a clearing. It was bigger—though not much—than a football field.

There were two canvas-draped pavilions, one at

each end of the field, both aflutter with flags. Several men milled about. They wore brightly colored tunics and tights, and most had swords strapped to their waists, though none, mercifully, had Day-Glo hair. They seemed divided into two groups, each centered around one of the pavilions. No, wait a minute. Deanna caught her breath. Centered around one of the two men, steadfastly ignoring each other, dressed in chain-mail armor.

"Knights," Deanna whispered, remembering the stories she had read about Arthur and Charlemagne and El Cid. Defend the weak and come to the aid of ladies in distress: she knew the code of chivalry. Well, *she* was a lady in distress!

"Nights?" Oliver asked. He made as if to stop her, but she sidestepped him.

"Knights," she repeated, more loudly, more confidently. She pushed a branch out of her way, stepping into the clearing. "Knights can help us."

"Nights?" she heard Oliver repeat. But he trusted her; he followed.

"Hello," she called, approaching the nearer group.

That knight, who was getting shin protectors strapped on over his chain mail, glanced at her, then returned his attention to his attendants.

"Ahm . . . Excuse me?" What if he spoke French? Come to that, what if he spoke English? That was no guarantee he'd understand her or she'd understand him: she remembered how her ninth-grade English class had studied Shakespeare's *A Midsummer Night's Dream,* and she had certainly not understood that. Her voice was beginning to fade. "Excuse me?"

The knight looked up again. "Well, come on, girl. Don't dawdle." She understood him perfectly, which made no sense at all. She decided not to worry about it. He waved her closer.

Deanna didn't look at Oliver for fear of seeing an I-told-you-so expression on his face. But she was aware of him walking beside her, warily evaluating the small crowd.

Gingerly she approached until she stood right before the knight.

He ignored her. He was a young man, though older than Oliver, and he had a droopy mustache that gave him a sad, whimsical look. His attendants were helping him get into metal gloves. Across the field, the other knight and his people were doing much the same.

"Ahm . . . " She cleared her throat. "Hello."

"You already said that." The knight slapped away the hands of one of his servants, who was too slow about tightening the wrist straps.

"Sorry, Sir Baylen," the attendant said.

"Here, give me that." The knight, Baylen, took the helmet one of the other men held. "Can't you see I'm busy?" he snapped at her.

"Well, yes, uhm, I'm sorry—"

"No time for that, no time for that. Just tell me what you have to tell me, then get out of the way. Look around you, girl, this is important business." He handed the helmet to a second attendant, who placed it on Baylen's head.

"Well, you see, ahm, Sir Baylen, I'm on a quest—"

"What?" The knight lifted his visor. "Can't hear a word with this thing on."

"Oh, I'm s—"

"Is this very important?"

"Yes, I'm afraid—"

"Speak up. A lot rides on what happens here today."

Deanna gulped, realizing the men were preparing to fight. A wrong to be righted? Blood feud? War? "I'm Deanna, and this is my friend, Oliver, and—"

"Friend?" Baylen lingered on the *f* and rolled the *r* as though that were the most ridiculous thing he had ever heard. Several of his attendants gave her sidelong glances also.

Deanna felt her cheeks grow warm. "Yes, you see, we're on a quest—"

"Oh, no, not another one of those." The knight let his visor drop. His voice came hollow and distant as he said, "See me about it afterward. Can't you see how important this is?" He started toward his horse—the other knight was mounted already—but turned back once. *"Friend,"* she heard him snort.

One of the attendants held the ornately caparisoned horse steady while another gave Sir Baylen a leg up. Yet another, scurrying forward with a lance that was twice as long as Deanna was tall, warned, "Coming through, miss."

"Oh, excuse—" She stepped out of his way and came down on the foot of another young man who was bringing a shield. "Out of the way please, miss," that one said.

"I'm so sor—"

Someone put a steadying hand to her elbow, and Deanna automatically turned to apologize.

"That's quite all right, my dear." This was an older man, a grandfatherly type dressed in rich, embroidered robes. "Perhaps we should step out of the way?"

"Oh, yes. Please."

He indicated a table that was set up between the two pavilions but off to the side, almost among the trees. Out of the knights' way, Deanna saw. She remembered a phrase from her reading: *out of the field of combat*. She shivered, recalling other phrases having to do with slaying and smiting and striking to the ground. Yield or die. That sort of thing.

"Drink of lemonade, my dear?" asked the grandfatherly type.

Startled, Deanna turned from watching the two knights, who had begun riding at each other from opposite corners of the field, their long lances held steady before them.

The old gentleman held out a silver goblet.

"Thank y—" she started to say, but the gentleman, looking beyond her, called: "Good show, Baylen!"

Deanna saw that the knights had passed each other. One—not the one to whom she had spoken—had dropped his lance and weaved a bit in his saddle but then regained his balance.

"Well done, eh?"

"Mmmm," Deanna murmured, taking a big swallow from her goblet to avoid having to say anything else when she had no idea what she was supposed to say.

The knights' attendants handed them both fresh lances, and they wheeled their horses about to come at each other again.

The grandfatherly man poured another lemonade. There were several pitchers and a great many goblets, but most of the table was occupied by three men, who sat at it scribbling away on heavy parchment scrolls.

Oliver looked warily at the offered goblet and shook his head.

"I don't believe I know you, do I, my dear?" the old man said to her. "You're not from near here?"

"No," Deanna said. "My name is Deanna, and I'm from Greeley, and his is Ol—"

"Greeley? Greeley? That's in Bretagne, isn't it?"

She took a deep breath, but before she could go on, he said: "I'm Sir Henri of Belesse. Pleased to meet you, Lady Deanna of Bretagne."

Whatever language they were all speaking, whether the old man in fact pronounced her name *Deanna* or *Dionne*—it came out sounding right to Deanna, which was an improvement over her French relatives. But *Bretagne?* "Actually, I'm not—"

He held up a hand to stop her, and she turned to view the knights. They were quickly closing the gap between them. The horses' hooves thundered, sending clumps of dirt flying. Closer. Closer. Deanna braced herself, but at the last second couldn't take it and closed her eyes.

"Ha!" Sir Henri shouted. "Did you see that?"

Deanna opened her eyes in time to see him give Oliver a hearty whack on the shoulder. She glanced at the field, ready to look away quickly in case of blood or obviously broken bones, but there was nothing worse than one of the knights chasing after his horse, the same who had almost been toppled in the previous run.

"Knocked Leonard clear out of the saddle!" their companion crowed. "Did you ever see the like?"

"No," Deanna admitted, which was certainly true. She checked to see Oliver's reaction.

He was holding his shoulder and looking at the old man's back with much the same expression she'd seen him use on the neighbors' dog. She put her hand on his arm. "Be polite," she whispered urgently. "Be pleasant."

He relaxed slightly, then nodded impatiently toward the forest.

Deanna shrugged helplessly.

One of the fallen knight's attendants had gotten hold of the horse by the bridle and brought it back to him. He scrambled back on, then once again faced his opponent, the knight Baylen, each of them armed with fresh lances.

Oliver stepped closer to her. "Does this go on all afternoon, or what?"

"Shhh."

He lowered his voice to a whisper. "Does this go on all afternoon, or what?"

She didn't like it any better, but she certainly couldn't handle this situation by herself; and if they didn't get help here, what were they going to do?

The knights got closer and closer.

"Come on," Sir Henri urged, and Deanna wondered what his connection was with all this: The wronged party? An arbitrator? What did he have riding on the outcome?

Another couple of seconds . . .

"Oh for two," the old man said.

"I beg your pardon?" asked Deanna.

"Zero to two. Baylen's favor. If Leonard doesn't do something soon, he might as well pack up and go home."

The knights met in a mighty crash. This time Leonard's lance snapped, and it was Baylen who almost lost his saddle.

Sir Henri slapped his thighs. "That's the way, Leonard! Now you're looking alive!"

"I thought you were for Baylen," Deanna said, understanding this less and less.

"Well, I can't very well be for either one: they're both my sons."

For a moment, Deanna had a vision of family misfortune of epic proportions, but then Sir Henri said, "Did you get that?" and she saw that he was addressing the men at the table, the ones writing on the scrolls. "What's going on?" she asked.

"Extra points for that, you know, breaking a lance. Leonard's not out of this game yet."

Deanna, watching Oliver, asked, "Game?"

"This is very exciting," Sir Henri said, reading one of the scrolls over the recorder's shoulders. "The last time that the challenger didn't score 'til the third round and then snapped his lance must have been . . . When was it, Ransom?"

"Thirty-eight, my Lord," one of the recorders answered. "Theobald the Grim against Ahern Three-Fingers."

"And that was an exhibition tournament."

"Excuse me," Deanna tried to interrupt.

"How about for their experience level? I mean this is only Leonard's fourth year."

"Let me see . . . "

"Excuse me," Deanna said again.

"What are the statistics for brothers in competition? How does that hold up to—"

"Excuse me." Deanna spoke so loudly that the old man stopped talking and the recorders stopped recording. Beyond the range of her voice, the knights closed in on each other again, this time on foot, carrying blunted swords.

"I thought there was something important going on here," she said. "Oliver and I are on a life-or-death mission, and we were told to wait because something important was going on here."

"There is." The old man's tone was considerably less grandfatherly; he was obviously miffed. "Just because we're keeping score and comparing statistics doesn't mean that this is unimportant."

"Well, then—" Deanna could see the recorders put their heads down and start scribbling away; obviously Baylen and Leonard, behind her, had begun round four. "What exactly are they fighting about?"

"Whose is the fairest lady."

"Fairest . . ." Deanna looked from him to Oliver, who was looking determinedly noncommittal about all this. ". . . lady?"

Sir Henri nodded. "You see, they both went off on quests—knights errant, don't you know?—and each came home betrothed to a foreign-born princess, and—"

"You mean they haven't even seen each other's lady?"

There must have been an edge to her voice, for Sir Henri seemed to lose some of his enthusiasm. "Well, I mean, not so much actually . . . this is, so to speak, not what you might in fact, *per se,* call physically—"

"No," Deanna said. "What you're saying is no. They're fighting over whose lady is the fairest, and neither has any idea what the other's lady looks like."

"Well, as a matter of fact, they don't know what their own ladies look like yet, either. That was the nature of their quests."

Deanna put her face in her hands.

"They'll be meeting them come Christmas. Which leaves them plenty of time, before then, to help you with your quest."

"I see." Did she want to get involved with people like this? Deanna straightened her shoulders. Good manners required a polite answer. "Thank you for all your help," she said, though he'd been no help at all.

"My pleasure, Lady Deanna." Sir Henri kissed her hand before she realized what he was up to. He didn't seem to notice that her cheeks flamed brightly. "Meanwhile, why don't you go up to the castle and wait for the boys to finish here?" He pointed in the direction which they would have taken had they continued on the path the elves had indicated. Now that she looked, she could see a tower over the trees.

She hesitated, and he said, "It's the only castle within several days' journey. Most people keep clear of the woods here. Said to be enchanted, don't you know?"

"Really?" she asked weakly.

"So why don't you and . . ." He looked at Oliver.

"This is Oliver." Because she'd had such bad luck introducing him as her friend, she decided that young ladies of this time must not wander around unchaperoned in the company of young male friends. She added: "My squire."

"Squire!" Sir Henri sputtered.

Even Oliver gave her a startled look.

But the old man got distracted by the knights' duel. "Good!" he bellowed. "Ransom, did you get that?" He turned back to Deanna. "Well, but you're Breton. I was forgetting."

"No—" Deanna started.

"So you just run ahead and introduce yourselves to my sister, Lady Marguerite. We'll be along shortly. Did you see that parry? Did everyone see that parry?"

Deanna whirled around and started walking.

In an instant Oliver had caught up. She waited for him to say "I told you so," but he said nothing. Almost to the castle, she finally couldn't take it anymore. "Well?" she demanded. "Go ahead, say it."

But what he said was "Why squire?"

It took her a moment to recover. "Why not squire?"

"Because squires attend knights, not ladies."

"I didn't know that," Deanna admitted.

"But that's what the word means."

Wonderful. She needed help to go on existing, and the fair folk gave her a walking dictionary. Deanna stopped and turned on him. They stood nose-to-nose because he was a small youth, as he had been a small cat. Which meant he wasn't as perfect as he thought. "I didn't know that," she repeated. "Who attends ladies?"

"Pages," he suggested.

"Thank you." She turned around and resumed walking. "Stop laughing at me," she said.

"I'm not laughing."

She looked at him and realized she couldn't be sure, one way or the other.

5 / Castle Belesse

The castle was not what Deanna had anticipated. She had assumed something along the lines of Sleeping Beauty's Castle at Disneyland, where she had gone with her parents last summer; but Sir Henri's family home was small as castles go and built of rough gray stone. No graceful spires and arches, only one stocky tower with a narrow little window high up off the ground. There was a moat, but it certainly wasn't deep enough for a moat monster, which was a major disappointment for her. She seemed to have been directed here. Was this where her watch had landed when she'd dropped it through the magic well? Or would she find someone here more helpful than Oliver—a champion who would rescue her and save the world as she knew it?

As soon as Deanna and Oliver crossed the drawbridge, they had to make room for a dusty man who appeared to be taking a group of pigs for a stroll around the unpaved courtyard.

"Keep up, Squeakers. Mind yer business, Patch.

Keep clear of the lady, all." He doffed his gray woolen cap, and Deanna curtsied, which may or may not have been the appropriate response to a pigman, and held her breath until they had passed, which certainly was appropriate.

"Nice place, huh?" she said, brushing dust off her gown.

"Hard to say." Oliver glanced around. "Looks like they might have mice."

Deanna wasn't sure what to make of that. But by then another man had come around the corner. He had a shaven head, dark bushy eyebrows, and a velvet gown of midnight blue, sprinkled with embroidered gold stars. He carried a staff with a fist-sized crystal ball. "Looks like your traditional wizard," she muttered to Oliver.

"The one with the frog?" he asked.

It took her a moment to remember. "Would you forget the frog?"

"You're the one—"

"Shh."

The man, headed for the entrance to the castle proper, had seen them. He did a double take, staring at Deanna. This was not, she sensed, someone who would put her mistakes in language down to being Breton.

"Greetings," he said, smiling, showing more teeth than a weekday-afternoon game-show host. "Welcome to Castle Belesse."

Inexplicably, she found herself pondering the question: *Would you buy a vowel from this man?* She took a step away. "No," she said.

The teeth disappeared. "No? Welcome to Castle Belesse—no?"

"Er, yes."

"Yes?" Decidedly cool now.

"Thank you," Oliver supplied.

The wizard's eyes shifted from her to him, back to her. He gave a tight smile, like Deanna's Aunt Verna, who suffered from chronic indigestion. "Hmm," he said. "Well. I'm Sir Henri's brother, Algernon."

"Deanna." She held out her hand.

Perhaps she was supposed to have recognized his name. In any case, she obviously wasn't supposed to offer a handshake. He stared at her outstretched hand, and after a moment she used it to indicate Oliver. "And this is Oliver, my page."

The wizard gave Oliver's sword the same long, meaningful gaze he had given her hand. "Not from anywhere near here," he observed.

"From Greeley."

"Ah! Greeley. Which is . . . "

She had been willing to tell Sir Henri, but she was darned if she was going to tell this character Algernon. "Across the sea."

He flashed that toothy game-show smile again. "Which sea?"

"Several of them actually. Is Lady Marguerite in? Sir Henri sent us." Which was true only in the strictest sense, but this wizard was making her desperately nervous.

He folded his arms across his chest. "Ah, the Lady Marguerite. I'm her brother, too."

But then another voice cut in: "I can take you to

see her—miss, sir." The speaker was a tall, skinny girl with a struggling goose tucked under her arm. "The lady's in her room, of course, this time of day. But she'll be glad for the company."

The wizard glared at the servant girl, but then he bowed to Deanna. "My pleasure," he murmured. "We must talk again at greater length, my Lady Deanna."

"If we must, we must," Deanna said, hoping she'd be long gone before that. She rushed to catch up with the goosegirl.

Oliver moved in beside her, which she knew by seeing him, never by hearing: his steps were quick and quiet, and his breathing never became labored as the goosegirl led them up several flights of steep stairs.

"Keep an eye out for that one," Deanna whispered.

Oliver shot her a quizzical look, mouthing the words: Eye out?

"He's the one." Oliver's persistent blank look was becoming infuriating. "The one who's going to find the watch and change history, like the fair folk warned."

"Algernon?" Oliver whispered. "How can you tell?"

"Well, just look at him."

He glanced back the way they had come. "But Deanna, he's not here."

"I mean, you can tell—*I* can tell—by the way he looks. He looks like a troublemaker. Trust me, Oliver. I know what I'm talking about."

"I trust you," Oliver said, with enough sincerity to make the hairs on her arms stand on end. Surely he didn't consider *her* the leader?

"That wizard." She raised her voice for the servant girl to hear, "Algernon. Is he a good wizard or a wicked one?"

"Oh, I couldn't ever say anything bad about Lord Algernon."

Couldn't? Deanna wondered, but before she could ask, the girl finally stopped in front of a heavy wooden door and rapped her knuckles against it.

"Visitors, Lady Marguerite."

Deanna heard no answer, but the girl pushed the door open, then curtsied at Deanna and Oliver. "Good day, miss." She covered a giggle with her hand. "Sir." And she scurried away down the hall, leaving them to enter the room or go back the way they had come.

The room was dimly lit. Heavy tapestries hung on the walls, floor to ceiling, blocking out all hint of sunlight if there were, in fact, windows behind them. There were a few candles placed on the various chests and tables in the room, giving the place the look and scent of a church between services. Except, of course, for the big bed in the center of the room. And the lady in it, surrounded by so many pillows it was hard to tell where they ended and she began.

Deanna curtsied. "Lady Marguerite," she said. "I'm sorry to bother you. We didn't realize you were ill."

"Nonsense, my dear," came the lady's faint voice from among the pillows. "I'm perfectly fit. It's just that direct sunlight is the kiss of death to one's complexion." But then, as though on second thought: "I don't look ill, do I?" Lady Marguerite pulled a mirror out from under one of the pillows. "Do you think I look ill?" she asked anxiously. "You don't see any age spots, do you?"

"No, no," Deanna assured her, though the room was so badly lit Lady Marguerite could have been a giant turnip for all Deanna could see. "You look fine."

"Are you sure?" the lady asked. "I don't have any bags under my eyes, do I? My friend Lady Rosamond said to rest silver teaspoons against my eyes five times a day to prevent dark circles and sagging, but I can't remember if she said to use a cold spoon or a warm spoon and she's gone to Normandy for her cousin's daughter's wedding. So I've been using both: cold spoons first and then warm spoons on Mondays, Wednesdays, and Fridays. And warm spoons first, then cold spoons on Tuesdays, Thursdays, and Saturdays. And on Sundays, I use the cold spoons first, then the warm ones, then the cold ones again. Do you know which it's supposed to be?"

"No, I'm sorry," Deanna said.

"You don't use spoons?"

"I'm afraid not."

"Hmm," Lady Marguerite said. But before she could ask anything else Oliver interrupted, saying, "Actually, we've never seen you look better."

Lady Marguerite, without stopping to consider that they had, in fact, never before seen her at all, got gigglish and giddy. "Why, what a sweet thing to say! Do you really think so? How delightful to have such a handsome young man say such a lovely thing."

Such a fuss, Deanna thought. She leaned to whisper into Oliver's ear, "You sly dog."

He gave a startled look, but Lady Marguerite didn't notice any of it.

"You must stay for lunch," she said. "I insist. The boys are out in the woods having their little joust, but they should be back any time now. I usually don't go down for lunch, but I'll make an exception for such charming company."

Charming company, my foot, Deanna thought. Once noticing him, Lady Marguerite hadn't taken her eyes off Oliver for a second. Deanna could have fallen out the window and Lady Marguerite would never have noticed.

"So you two run down to the Hall while my maid gets me ready." She tugged on the embroidered bell pull that lay across one of her pillows.

"Thank you," Oliver said, with a smile that Deanna had to admit was maybe the slightest bit charming. He had never smiled at *her* like that.

Deanna recovered enough to remember to curtsy before leaving. "Hmpfh!" she said to Oliver as they started back down the stairs.

"What?"

"Nothing. I'm glad she suggested lunch. I'm starving."

"You are?" he asked with such alarm that Deanna had to explain: "It's an expression, Oliver."

"Expression?"

"Never mind."

If Lady Marguerite was going to flirt with strangers, she probably deserved somebody like Oliver.

* * *

They got lost trying to find the dining hall. But apparently Lady Marguerite sent word to watch out for them, and eventually the servants came and found them.

How embarrassing, Deanna thought, being led through several storage rooms and around the stables. They weren't even in the right building. Three men patching a garden wall pointed down the corridor as though she and Oliver couldn't find the Hall even with an escort.

The Hall itself was almost as big as her school cafeteria. It smelled more like a picnic cabin, though—all smoky from roasting meat. Dogs barked and fought over scraps. Little children, finished eating, played tag among the tables while the adults had to come close to shouting to be heard over the noise of talking and laughing and servants cleaning up after the meal.

The man who had been walking the pigs in the courtyard was sitting at the table nearest to the door, and he stood, removing his cap once more, when he saw Deanna. She curtsied once again, and the others sitting at that table—field laborers, by their clothes and grimy appearance—nudged each other and grinned. Okay, so she'd done something wrong again. Dumb elves. As long as they could change a cat to a human and make her understand medieval French, you'd think they could have used up a little bit more of their magic to give her pointers on proper castle etiquette.

"There they are," Sir Henri called, motioning Deanna and Oliver to the head table.

Immediately Lady Marguerite made room for them

next to her. Everyone sat on one side of the table, so that the food could be served more easily. The wizard, Algernon, was on the end, then Sir Henri, and their sister, Lady Marguerite. Deanna knew what their hostess had in mind when she patted the seat next to her, but Oliver didn't, or he pretended not to: he kept to Deanna's right side so that Deanna ended up between them. Next to Oliver sat a bearded young man who had to be Leonard, whose face they'd never seen beneath his helmet; the droopy-mustached Baylen sat on the end. Judging by Leonard's sullen and single-minded attention to the meal in front of him, and by Baylen's self-satisfied smile, Deanna guessed that—snapped lance or no—Leonard had lost the morning's match.

Lady Marguerite looked older than she had appeared in her dimly lit room, though not so old as Deanna had anticipated from her preoccupation with bags under the eyes. She wore a satin gown that was low-cut enough that Deanna wondered how it stayed up, and more jewelry than Deanna had ever before seen on any one person. She craned around Deanna to ask Oliver, "So, did you have any trouble finding the Hall?"—which had to be the world's dumbest question, considering that she and Oliver had set out first, and not gotten there 'til all the others at the table had already finished with their food. (With the possible exception of Leonard, who in any case seemed more interested in sticking his knife into his meat than actually picking it up and eating it.) So she couldn't help but answer, "No. No trouble, thank you." And she flashed a smile that she hoped was at least as charming as Oliver's.

It was wasted, because Lady Marguerite wasn't looking at her. "I hope you brought your appetite," she told Oliver.

He paused to consider. "Yes," he said slowly. He glanced at Deanna for reassurance and she gave a half nod. "I'm starving. That's an expression."

"Yes," Lady Marguerite said. "Good." She batted her eyelashes at him. "Now this is embarrassing, but I'm sorry: I don't believe I know your name."

Oliver was warily watching the serving boy, who was ladling stew onto their plates.

Lamb, Deanna guessed by the smell of it. Yum, one of her favorite things. Right up there with Spam and brussels sprouts and lukewarm milk. Oliver didn't look too happy about it either. "I'm Deanna," she said, since Oliver wasn't saying anything, "and this is Oliver. He's my—" She remembered the look Algernon had given Oliver's sword and had a suspicion pages might not carry weapons, so she lowered her voice. "—my brother." Which was ridiculous since they didn't look anything alike. And in any case she must have lowered her voice too much, for the others at the table seemed to think she hadn't finished her sentence.

"Squire," Sir Henri said.

"Page," Algernon said.

"Friend," Baylen said.

All at once.

Leonard looked up from poking his stew. "General all-'round fellow, eh?" he observed.

"We're on a quest," Deanna told them. "And we, uh . . ."

"Can't tell you any more than that," Oliver finished.

"Ah!" everybody said knowingly. Except for Leonard, who looked bored and returned his attention to skewering his vegetables. And Algernon, who gave her a grin as though they shared a secret joke.

"Well," Deanna said, turning away from him to the two brothers, "so how did the joust go?"

"Very nicely," Baylen said.

"Cheap, miserable horse couldn't keep its footing," Leonard said.

"Don't you care for lamb, dear?" Lady Marguerite asked Oliver.

Deanna saw that he was sitting with his hands in his lap, looking disconsolate. "Care for . . . lamb?" he repeated noncommittally.

"Do you like rabbit?"

His face brightened. "Whenever I can get one."

Lady Marguerite snapped her fingers for a servant to pass the platter of roast rabbit.

Deanna had a sudden awful thought. "It's really too bad you couldn't attend your nephews' joust," Deanna told her. (Did Oliver know anything about table manners?) "It was really quite exciting." (What if he just stuck his face into the plate?)

"Excitement's not good for the skin," Lady Marguerite said. "Rush of the blood to the face and all that. It ages one. Isn't the rabbit cooked right for you, dear?"

"Do you have anything, maybe, *not* cooked?" Oliver asked.

Deanna gulped.

"Grapes?" Lady Marguerite reached for a bowl. "Peaches?"

Oliver stood abruptly, scraping his chair against the floor, so that everyone turned to stare. "Actually I'm not starving after all. I think I'll go for a walk in the garden."

"But . . ." Deanna said.

"But . . ." Lady Marguerite said.

Oliver turned and left.

Leonard moved in closer to Deanna and flashed a grin almost as reassuring as Algernon's. "Strange, that all-'round fellow of yours."

Deanna feigned preoccupation with her lamb stew. It was cold by now, with the grease congealing, which made it even less appetizing. She took a bite, which settled in a hard lump between her chest and her stomach.

Sir Henri leaned forward. "Leonard," he said, "Ransom's devised a new saddle grip that might help—"

"Oh, who cares?" Lady Marguerite snapped. She got up and swept out of the Hall.

Baylen stretched, then stood. "Anyway," he said, "*I* won."

"Cheap horse," Leonard answered. But it seemed an instinctive reaction, with little feeling. He was still smiling at Deanna.

"Now, Baylen, that's not the proper sporting attitude." Sir Henri threw his arm around his older son's shoulder and the two of them left the room, discussing point spreads and handicaps.

So here she was, abandoned, sitting between Leonard, who had his arm around the back of the bench behind her, and the wizard Algernon, who was sidling over next to her. Appearances to the contrary, Leonard was engaged—betrothed, they called it here—and had just fought his brother on his fiancée's behalf. Obviously Deanna was misinterpreting his intentions: she wasn't familiar with this time, with their social customs. He was just being friendly, she told herself. Algernon, on the other hand . . .

"Leonard," she said, thinking he might be the solution to her quest, if she could just get him alone to talk to him about it, "how about if you show me around Castle Belesse so I don't get lost again?"

Leonard looked surprised, then pleased, then self-satisfied. "Certainly," he said. "See you around, Uncle Algernon."

The wizard nodded, never taking his gaze from Deanna. "Later," he assured her.

6 / Leonard

Leonard and Deanna passed the dusty pig keeper on their way out of the Hall. He stood, bowing and removing his cap as he seemed to do every time he saw her. "Miss," he mumbled.

Behind his back, the other servants at the table snickered and rolled their eyes and nudged one another in the ribs.

Why, they're laughing at him as much as at me, Deanna thought, and to save his pride curtsied even though she was fairly certain by now that ladies of her (apparent) social standing didn't curtsy to men of his (obvious) social standing.

"Miss," he repeated, and this time she got the impression he was about to say more, but Leonard hustled her out of the room. "So," he said, "how about if I show you—"

"The gardens," she interrupted. That's where Oliver had said he was going and she didn't like having him out of her sight. There was no telling what he'd get himself into without her.

"All right. The gardens, then." Leonard had his arm entwined with hers, which she didn't care for, and which made walking awkward, but she put it down to French social customs of the—what was this?—tenth or eleventh century. "I'm so pleased that you and your . . . quest partner have come to Castle Belesse," he started. "You know, I—"

"Thank you. Tell me about your uncle."

"My uncle?"

"What's he do, just say magic words and magic happens? Or does he use things? You know, bats' wings, lizards' teeth, or something?"

Leonard curled his lip in disgust. "You mean does my Uncle Algernon go around plucking body parts from the local wildlife?"

"Or something?"

Leonard shrugged.

Boy, he was being helpful. "Amulets? Charms?"

Again he shrugged.

"Mysterious things that come out of nowhere that you don't know what they are or how they're used, maybe about this big, with numbers on it and a white leather strap?"

"Who knows? I don't know."

"Well, is he a good wizard?"

"Good?"

The question hadn't come out the way she had intended. "I mean, is he good at what he does? His spells work and all that?"

"Well, yes, I suppose. He can make people disappear."

"People disappear?"

"Well, not important people. Here, watch your step." The garden had a lower level, and they had to go down a couple of steps. There was a metal handrail, and the steps were made of large, even slabs of stone, but Leonard moved behind her, putting one hand on her elbow and the other around her waist as though guiding her down a treacherous mountain trail.

Again the thought crossed her mind that this was terribly awkward and that she could manage better without him. Algernon could make people disappear, and Leonard shrugged it off because they weren't important people.

"We wouldn't want you falling and hurting your lovely self," Leonard said.

"You're too kind," she murmured, a phrase she'd heard her mother use with Dad's cousin Sid, who had a tendency to put lamp shades on his head and say things for which he'd have to call the following day and apologize. She leaned to one side to force Leonard to let go. "Now about your Uncle Algernon—"

He whirled her around and started kissing her hand. "Your skin is fair as a lily, kissed by the first blush of dawn."

She snatched her hand away. "Stop that."

"Your eyes are like limpid pools."

"They are not." She was getting frightened now.

"Your lips . . . ah, your cherry lips . . . If I might just once touch—"

He reached as though to lay a finger across her lips, and she slapped his hand down. "Back off, you," she warned. But her voice shook, her heart pounded. There was a wooden bench on the path, and she stepped behind it, to force Leonard to keep his distance.

"Your lips say *no,* but your eyes say *yes,*" he told her.

"My eyes say no such thing."

He began circling the bench. "You're beautiful when you're angry," he said.

But she circled also, and managed to keep the bench between them. "No, I'm not. And what about your fiancée?"

"The betrothal's off." He feinted to the right, then lunged to the left, and she just managed to pull back so that his hand closed on empty air instead of around her wrist.

"The betrothal's off?" she repeated, to keep him talking, to keep him distracted. And she had thought Algernon was dangerous. "Why?"

"Because I challenged Baylen but he won the joust. That means his lady is fairer than mine was. I'm not going to be stuck marrying someone who makes Baylen come off better than me."

"That doesn't make any sense." Deanna thought he looked as though he was considering climbing over the bench, and she didn't know what she'd do if he did that. She had no idea how fast she could run in her long gown and thin slippers. "And anyway, suppose Baylen's lady is fairer than me?"

"She won't be. She can't be. And, anyway, to be on the safe side, I won't challenge him."

Thanks a lot. She stepped away as he reached over

the bench but wasn't fast enough: Leonard caught hold of her wrists. "Let go of me," she cried. She jerked back, and her tall hat slipped down over her eyes.

"Don't toy with my emotions, icy goddess of love." Leonard put a knee on the seat of the bench and tried to draw her toward him.

She dug her heels into the grass and leaned backward.

"I love the fire in your eyes," he insisted.

Her foot slipped in the grass. He was still pulling on her arms, so that she lost her balance. She fell across the back of the bench and he, with one knee still on the seat, was unable to counteract the effect of her weight. The bench tipped, then rolled: Leonard ended up flat on his back with the bench on top of him and Deanna on top of the bench.

"My lady," he gasped. "My lady, you're squashing me!"

Deanna became aware that someone was standing next to her. She could see boots, but she was having a hard enough time figuring which way was up, never mind who it was standing there. She brushed the hat back.

Leonard's face was turning an interesting shade of purple as she pushed on the bench, trying to lift herself up. "My lady! Stop. You're killing me."

Oliver stooped down where Deanna could see him. "Does he really mean that?" he asked, indicating Leonard. "Or is that just an expression?"

"If I'm lucky, he means it," Deanna said.

Oliver nodded. "Are you just . . ." She could see

him groping for exactly the right words. ". . . amusing yourself? Or do you need help?"

"I could use a hand up."

Oliver pulled her to her feet. "Are you injured?" he asked. "Have you been harmed?"

Leonard rolled the bench off himself. "No, no," he answered sulkily. "Don't worry about me. I'm quite all right."

"I wasn't worried about you," Oliver answered evenly. "I was asking about Deanna."

Leonard got to his feet. He stood directly in front of Oliver, who, being considerably shorter, had to look up at him. "Sort of an idiot, aren't you?" Leonard growled.

"I'm not the one who was lying on the ground with a park bench on my chest," Oliver pointed out.

Leonard snorted. But he must have become aware of how he looked, all rumpled, with grass and leaves stuck to him. And perhaps he became aware too of Oliver's hand, resting on the hilt of his elfin sword. Leonard glanced at Deanna, gave a curt bow, snorted at Oliver again, then strode away as though he had more important things to think of.

"Oh, Oliver," Deanna said, unable to resist the impulse to hug him. Maybe he could help her save the world after all. "You're a treasure."

"I am?" He sounded a little confused but was obviously pleased that she was pleased.

She linked her arm with his and started walking him back to the castle. It must be late afternoon and he wouldn't have had anything to eat since breakfast at the farm. "What we've got to do is find you some food. I'm sure if we go to the kitchen—"

"No," said Oliver. "I've already found food."

"Oh?" she asked innocently. "What?"

He gave her that same level look he had given Leonard. "I don't think you really want to know."

Deanna opened her mouth, closed it. Opened it again, closed it again. Let go of his arm. "Right. Well." She readjusted the hat, which had suddenly developed a tendency to lean to one side. She kept on walking, without looking at him. He looked so real, she kept forgetting. "You came just in time, you know."

"I didn't know. What happened?"

"Well, you heard Leonard and Baylen were fighting to see whose fiancée is the fairest. It turns out since Leonard lost so badly, he figures his lady must be a real dog, so he wants to replace her with me."

Oliver stopped and stared at her. *"Leonard is marrying a dog?"*

Deanna sighed. She reminded herself that he had come to her rescue twice already today. She sighed again. "It's just another expression, Oliver."

7 / Algernon

What we've got to do," Deanna told Oliver as they climbed the garden stairs back to the higher level, "is find that watch fast and get back home. I have a bad feeling about that wizard Algernon. If he gets to the watch before we do, we'll never get it back in time." Oh, why hadn't the elves been more helpful? Just because it wasn't their lives that were on the line . . .

"Maybe he has it already," Oliver said.

"No." Oh, surely it was more than wishful thinking. "No, he can't."

They stepped onto the packed earth of the courtyard, and she spied Algernon. "Speaking of the devil . . ." she murmured.

"Who was?" Oliver asked, even as Algernon, hanging around the front door as though waiting for them to return, caught sight of them.

"We were." Deanna lowered her voice as the wizard approached.

"No, we weren't," Oliver said, without lowering his. "We were talking about Algernon."

The wizard heard that and smiled, a smile involving only his lips, never his eyes. *Watch out,* she told herself.

"You were talking about me?" Algernon asked in a pleasant enough voice that nevertheless set goose bumps surfacing on her arms. "What a coincidence. I was just thinking about you." Incredibly, the smile broadened. "I don't believe in coincidence, do you?"

Deanna's heart thudded guiltily, blocking her throat, blocking any answer.

"If there is no such thing as coincidence," Oliver asked him, "why would there be a word for it?"

Algernon shot him a glare which was no doubt meant to be withering. But by the time he returned his attention to Deanna, the lump in her throat was dissolving, never mind the peculiar glint in the wizard's eyes. "On the contrary," she managed to tell him in a wonderfully grown-up voice, "I've recently found that fantastic coincidences happen all the time. It's logic and rational explanations I no longer believe in."

His lips twitched condescendingly. "How interesting. Have you, by chance, read Aristotle on the subject?" He started again without even giving her time to shake her head. "I have an early manuscript of his. I think you'd find *that* fascinating."

"Oh, that sounds very exciting," Deanna said. *Exciting* was her mother's catchall word. Deanna suspected her mother used it when she hadn't been listening and wasn't sure what she was supposed to say. "Very exciting, indeed." She was feeling self-confident and in control and in another second might even start giggling.

But Algernon was looking at her with those dark eyes of his that somehow seemed to sparkle, and there was something wrong here, though she couldn't say what, and—as though she were thinking about someone else—it occurred to her that she didn't have the strength to look away from whatever it was that sparkled and flashed in the wizard's eyes. "Fine," he said from far, far away. "It's right up in the tower room I use for my experiments. I'm sure you'll find all of it 'exciting.' " And the lights that had no business being in his eyes swirled and tightened, drawing her in, just as he was drawing her in, pulling her toward the castle. Her body moved sluggishly, as though wading through water, so that she didn't even feel the pressure of the wizard's fingers, though she could see the indentations they made in her arm. *People disappear,* she remembered Leonard telling her. Leonard? she asked herself. *Leonard?* Did she know a *Leonard?* She let the wizard guide her steps.

Someone had caught hold of her other arm. She realized that when the wizard was pulled up short and turned to look slightly beyond her. Deanna fought the thick air that weighed down her entire body. A youth was standing there, his long fingers wrapped around her wrist. Dark hair framed a face that looked as though it never smiled, but he had pretty green eyes. There was something wrong with those eyes, too, but she couldn't quite say what. *Too?* she thought. *Too?* Absently, she wondered who he was.

"We'll return shortly, boy," she heard her good friend Algernon tell him.

If her body wasn't being so slow to respond, she would already have turned back to the castle. But the youth was faster than she was. He was faster than Algernon was. Without releasing Deanna's wrist, he grabbed the wizard's free arm. His voice came from as far away as Algernon's. "We travel together," he said silkily.

Did they?

"Not this time." Algernon tried to jerk away but couldn't break his grip. He narrowed his eyes at the youth—Oliver: she knew that!—and directed the sparkling whirlpools at him.

Perhaps the wizard could only work his spell on one person at a time, Deanna thought, for she found she had cut through the thickness around her. Suddenly she was moving in real time instead of slow motion, and the fuzziness was gone from inside her head. "Let go of me," she cried, twisting in Algernon's grip. She kicked his leg, trying to distract him before he caught Oliver up in his magic.

Algernon kept hold of her arm (Oliver had her other arm and one of Algernon's—to anyone watching, she thought, they would have looked like an impromptu ring-around-the-rosy), but the wizard gave all his attention to Oliver. The lights in his eyes whirled faster and faster. Sweat beaded on his forehead. The veins in his neck were distended and the tense line of his jaw showed that his teeth were clenched in concentration.

Oliver made no attempt to break away. His eyes, which always looked too long, too deep, never left Algernon's. And it was Algernon, finally, who wilted, who released Deanna first. Slowly Oliver uncurled his fingers from around the wizard's forearm.

Algernon stepped back away from him. Subdued, he glanced at Deanna, too fast for her to avoid his eyes, but the unnatural glint was gone. "Who are you?" he asked, sounding shaken. "That's worked on every person . . ."

Deanna, looking at him sidelong, saw it hit him. "*What* are you?"

Nothing flickered across Oliver's bland face. Deanna felt a chill spread up her own back. For a moment she could see nothing that was human in Oliver's expression.

They stood there evaluating each other, Oliver impassively, Algernon with fury on his face, neither one ready to give an inch and both willing to stand there all day to prove it, and it was Baylen who saved the day.

"Uncle Algernon," Sir Henri's elder son called from the doorway of the stable.

Algernon turned, slowly, as though to indicate he'd keep on glaring at Oliver if pressing business didn't interfere.

Baylen, who looked as though he'd been winding

himself up for another bellow, waved for the wizard to join him. "That horse with the broken leg," he shouted.

Algernon spared one more look of disdain for Oliver and Deanna, then strode away.

A horse with a broken leg. Two summers ago Deanna had read all the novels she could find about horses. She knew what was done with a horse with a broken leg, and it figured they'd call Algernon to do it.

Watching him walk toward the stable, she found herself shaking over what he had been able to do to her will. She also found herself avoiding Oliver's eyes as fastidiously as she had avoided Algernon's. Oliver wasn't human. She kept forgetting because the fair folk had done such a good job in making him look like one. What was going on in his mind? She'd never know. Algernon's spell had had no effect on him—which was good, which had saved her from . . . who knows what? But it also showed that she'd never, ever be able to take things for granted. She couldn't assume she understood Oliver, couldn't try to guess how he'd react in any given situation. *Stop it,* she told herself. After all, he had just rescued her from the wizard. She forced herself to look directly at him. "Are you all right?" she asked, her voice a little squeak.

He looked at her coldly, which did nothing for her sense of unease. Cats were hunters, she recalled suddenly. Perhaps he was evaluating her weaknesses. Her unease teetered on the edge of fear. *Stop it,* she repeated to herself. Oliver wouldn't even be here except that he had tried to save her when she'd been pulled into the well.

"Why, there you are!" Lady Marguerite's voice chirped, coming up from behind them. "I've been looking all over for you."

Oliver turned, and something about the shift of muscles or the way the light fell across his cheek . . . The alien quality was hidden, or gone.

Lady Marguerite climbed the garden steps into the courtyard. Despite the exuberance of her greeting, she sounded out of breath, a bit frazzled even. She was dressed in a long-sleeved gown, with gloves and a shawl and a wide-brimmed hat to protect her from the sun. She must have been wandering around the garden for some time. There were bits of twigs and leaves trailing from the hem of her gown and stuck to the scarf around her hat. Her forehead was damp and smudged. But her gaze had lit on Oliver, and her face glowed. "Well," she said, looking down to Oliver's hand on Deanna's wrist, "so how are you enjoying your stay so far? I hope you found the garden to your liking."

Oliver let go of Deanna. As though unsure what to do with himself, he momentarily rested his hand on his sword hilt, then crossed his arms. "The garden is a good place for eating lunch," he said.

"A picnic!" Lady Marguerite hooked her arm through his and started walking him into the castle, never checking to see if Deanna was following. "What a splendid idea! I do so love picnics. Except for the sun, of course." She laughed gaily, holding on to Oliver's arm and tipping her head to one side coquettishly.

Deanna took a step. Found she was steadier than she would have thought. Took another step. Behind them, she imitated Lady Marguerite's gestures. Boy, Oliver was eating all this attention up. *Traitor!* she thought.

"Let me show you to the rooms I've had prepared for you," their hostess said, never including Deanna with a glance. "I hope you stay. It's so pleasant to have someone with fresh ideas around the place."

Uh-huh.

Deanna rubbed her wrist where Oliver's fingernails had come close to breaking her skin, and followed the two of them up the stairs, whether they knew she was there or not.

8 / *Afternoon*

Up stairs, through the Great Hall, up more stairs, along a corridor. The more they ignored her, the farther behind Deanna trailed as Lady Marguerite continued to chatter and laugh and cling to Oliver's arm. It wasn't fair. Oliver was supposed to help *her*. She couldn't handle this stupid quest on her own. *Turn around,* she wished at his back. *Notice me*. What was the matter with him?

Behind her, someone cleared his throat.

Deanna gasped and whirled around.

But it was only the pigman. Without his pigs for the moment, thank goodness.

Deanna held her hand over her racing heart as he took off his cap and slapped it against his leg, producing a cloud of dust. "Miss," he said.

"Sir." She curtsied and made to continue down the hall. Lady Marguerite and Oliver were just turning around a corner.

"Miss," the pigman repeated more insistently.

Just what she didn't need: someone else to take a sudden interest in her, but at least she had an excuse. "I'm sorry," she called back over her shoulder. "I can't stop."

She rounded the corner at a run and collided with someone. Leonard. He reeled back, but recovered before she did. He held a bright bouquet of wildflowers out to her. "A thousand apologies for startling you," he said, bowing. "A thousand more for frightening you in the garden."

Without acknowledging him, she tried to pass, but he grabbed her hand and dropped to his knees. "Forgive me!" he cried.

"I forgive you," she said, to get him to let go of her hand. "Don't do it again."

"I won't." He pressed his other hand, the one with the flowers, to his heart. "My lady, I swear my undying devotion—"

"Yes, thank you, go away." She tugged at her hand but couldn't get it free.

"Take these flowers," he said, "as a token of my love for you. Take them and hold them in your hand, as I hold you in my heart."

She took the flowers. "Now let go of my hand, Leonard."

He stood, then kissed her fingers, and then, finally, let go. "I'll count the moments until next I see your fair face." He bowed and backed away.

She didn't dare turn her back on him, so she watched until he disappeared around the corner. With a sigh, she again faced the direction she had seen Lady

Marguerite and Oliver going, sure in her heart that they had continued on without her.

Not only had they waited for her, but Baylen and his father had joined them. Baylen nodded in the direction Leonard had gone, rolled his eyes, and shook his head. Deanna felt her face go a hot red with humiliation.

Sir Henri didn't seem to notice. "Splendid," he said. "Splendid, you and Leonard hitting it off so well." He beamed proudly. "But now, tell us about this quest of yours. Can we help?"

Oh, yes, she thought, *please.* She wanted nothing more than to dump this whole mess in somebody else's lap. But then there was Algernon. Sir Henri's brother. Baylen's and Leonard's uncle. Who made people—albeit unimportant people—disappear. How much did she dare tell them? If Algernon learned what it was that she was looking for, then he might get to it first. And she couldn't very well tell them to trust her, a complete stranger, and not their relative. The more she thought about it, the more her head began to spin.

"Lady Deanna?" Sir Henri said.

"We're looking for something . . ." she said slowly, ". . . small . . ."

Sir Henri nodded as though to encourage her to go on.

She bit her lip and wondered if she had said too much already.

"Small things are generally harder to find than large things," Baylen observed.

Boy, that was helpful. "This would have been lost in or near the pond that's in the clearing in the forest. But I have reason to believe that it's been brought back here."

Baylen said, "We were in the forest this morning."

"Yes?" Deanna said breathlessly.

"We didn't find anything." Baylen turned to his father. "Did we find anything?"

"I didn't find anything," Sir Henri said.

"We didn't find anything," Baylen repeated.

Deanna sighed.

"But," Sir Henri said, "if it's to be found, we'll find it. How about if you and Marguerite go off and do whatever it is that you women go off and do, and Baylen, young Oliver, and I will start this quest of yours."

"Oh," said Lady Marguerite. "Must you?"

Meanwhile, Deanna prickled under the comment about women, but after all that was what she had been looking for: to hand this over to someone else. She looked warily at Oliver, who said nothing.

"Trust us," Sir Henri said jovially, throwing one arm around Baylen's shoulder and the other around Oliver's.

After all, she thought, the fair folk had specifically sent Oliver to help her, so maybe this was what they had intended. "Thank you," she said. Then, choosing her words carefully, "The only thing is that this is sort of a secret quest, so you can't tell anybody about it."

Sir Henri put his finger to his lips to indicate they were sealed.

"Go with them," Deanna told Oliver so that he would cooperate, "and do whatever they tell you."

He nodded solemnly.

I hope, she thought, watching the three of them walk down the hall together, *oh, I hope that was the right decision.*

The afternoon dragged miserably. Lady Marguerite kept trying to pump Deanna for information about Oliver: Was he always so quiet, what were his interests, did he enjoy the company of older women? That sort of thing.

Deanna tried to find out more about Castle Belesse and the people who lived there.

"It's just me and my brothers, Henri and Algernon," Lady Marguerite said. "And the boys, of course. Their poor mother's gone now. And there're the servants naturally. Actually, it's a very small castle."

"Any bigger and I'd have to drop bread crumbs," Deanna said.

Lady Marguerite look startled. "Well," she said, "I suppose if you really wanted to . . ."

It was eerily like trying to talk to Oliver. And how was Oliver doing? she wondered over and over. If he found the watch, surely he'd know enough to come straight back, wouldn't he? Besides, she found she missed his company. Everything was so strange here: the colorful tapestries that covered all the walls, the flags and banners that snapped in the wind, the stone floors and incredibly high ceilings that made her voice resonate as though she were in a cathedral. But as strange as all this was to her, it had to be stranger yet to Oliver. And if he was the closest thing she had to a friend here, she was the closest thing *he* had to a friend *anywhere*.

Lady Marguerite insisted that Deanna join her in her apartments, where she spent the rest of the afternoon weaving a tapestry that she said was Hannibal crossing the Alps. Some of the women servants joined them to work on their own projects: embroidery or mending. They were all amazed that Deanna didn't know how to sew and insisted on teaching her. Deanna gazed out the window and watched the sun get lower and lower in the sky and wondered if she had made the wrong decision. "Was Algernon in the forest this morning?" she asked.

"That's hard to say," Lady Marguerite answered. "Algernon comes and goes. Why don't you ask him?"

"Maybe I will," Deanna said. She was sure she'd made the wrong decision.

Late in the afternoon, Leonard joined them. He brought a mandolin, which he played softly, but at least he didn't say anything embarrassing.

By evening she could make passable buttonholes; but while buttonholes were nice, they were hardly in the same class as saving human civilization. On the other hand, surely Oliver had everything under control. Surely. She hoped.

Oh, Oliver, she thought as she went back to her room to freshen up before the evening meal, *be there. Please be there.*

He wasn't.

9 / Evening

Someone, *someone*—if she had three guesses, they'd all be Leonard—someone had put a potted rosebush outside her door. Deanna unsnagged her gown from it, then went inside and sat down on the edge of her bed in exhaustion. "Freshen up," they had said, as though it weren't her very life that was at stake. Lady Marguerite, after quizzing her on what might be Oliver's favorite color, had announced that she would change for supper. They were all supposed to meet in the Great Hall. Deanna threw down the silly conical hat in frustration.

Someone tapped on the door.

Oliver! she thought. But before she could say anything, Baylen's voice called, "Lady Deanna?"

She told herself that the sinking sensation she felt was due to her need to compare notes with Oliver, to see what he had found out, and perhaps lay new plans. "Yes? What is it?"

Baylen entered. She still thought his droopy mustache gave him a romantic, melancholy air, but she had long since come to the conclusion that all of Castle Belesse's inhabitants were at least a little loopy. He said, "Father said to stop by when it was time to eat so you don't get lost getting to the Hall again."

"Thank you." *Mr. Tact.* "Did you find anything?"

"Find," he said, "anything?"

It was difficult for her to keep from shouting. "My quest."

"Oh," he said. "That. We didn't get started yet."

This time she didn't even try to keep her voice level. "What do you mean, you didn't get started yet? You've been gone all afternoon."

"Yes, but Father wanted to test Oliver out first. See how good he is with a sword, that sort of thing. Why? Is there some rush with this quest thing?"

"Yes, of course there's a rush—what do you mean your father wanted to test how good he is with a sword?" she shouted all in one breath. She had a sudden awful thought. "You don't mean your father challenged him to a sword fight?"

Baylen nodded.

"Is he all right?" Deanna's heart pounded hard enough to hurt.

"Your Oliver? Sure. It was a friendly match. No training, but he's got good fighter's instincts—always lands on his feet."

Idiot, she thought, now that she knew Oliver was safe. And just what did Baylen mean by *Your Oliver*?

Baylen glanced out into the corridor. "Here he comes. Father set me to watch over him once he got sick."

"Who got sick?" Deanna asked, hoping, though it wasn't nice, that Baylen meant Sir Henri. But one look at Oliver answered her. For someone who was pale to begin with, he had no color at all, and his hair was damp around the edges as though he'd just rinsed his face.

"Him," Baylen said. "Been sicker than a dog most of the afternoon." He didn't see the look Oliver shot behind his back at that. "Maybe something you ate," he suggested.

That didn't bear thinking about at all. "Are you all right?" Deanna asked. Oliver didn't look too steady on his feet.

He nodded, his eyes looking overly large in his white and pinched face.

Baylen clapped him heartily on the shoulder. "Well, ready for supper, then?"

It wouldn't take much, Deanna thought, for Oliver to either throw up or go for Baylen's throat. "You know," she said, "maybe it'd be a good idea to skip supper this once. Oliver needs time for his stomach to settle, and I had a bigger lunch than usual so I'm not hungry at all. Why don't you thank your family for us, but tell them we'd rather not eat?"

"I don't know." Baylen scratched his belly reflectively. "Aunt Marguerite's not going to be too well pleased."

Deanna could imagine. She smiled and stayed where she was.

Baylen shrugged. "Right, then."

She waited for him to leave, then turned to Oliver. "Why didn't you look for the watch?" she demanded.

"You said to go with them and do what they said," he pointed out.

It was true, and he looked so sick and weak she relented. "I think you better lie down. Come on, let's get you back to your room." She put her arm around him, afraid that he might faint or collapse on the way, but found that he was steadier than he appeared. He jumped, startled at her touch, and after that it seemed somehow impolite to withdraw her arm. She escorted him to his chamber halfway down the corridor, embarrassed to death and hoping he couldn't tell.

"There you go," she said cheerfully as he got onto the bed. He didn't go under the covers but just curled up on top, looking miserable. "Anything I can get you?"

"Like what?"

"I don't know. Water? A blanket?" *Take two aspirin and call me in the morning,* she thought wryly. They didn't even have aspirin here. What if he was *really* sick?

He shook his head. "Why aren't you going to supper?"

"I thought it'd be a good chance to take a look in the wizard's room, while everybody's in the Hall. Explore."

Oliver sat up. "Not alone."

She couldn't tell if it was a question or a statement. "Yes, alone. You're in no shape to come along."

Oliver paused to reflect on her wording. "I'm well enough." He stood gingerly. He swayed a bit, blinked those big green eyes, then started for the door.

"Oliver, stay."

It had never worked when he was a cat, and it didn't work now. He held the door, waiting. "Darn you," she said. But time was running out. Tomorrow would be too late.

The wizard had said he lived in the tower, and that was easy to find: all they had to do to keep track was stick their heads out the windows—to the end of the corridor, up a flight of stairs, down another, around a couple of corners, through a columned gallery, around one corner, up a long curved stairway inside the tower itself, and they were there.

There was no handle or latch or lock on the door. Apparently you just pushed the door and walked in. That wasn't what she had expected. She didn't know what she had expected, but this wasn't it. Deanna straightened her shoulders, took a deep breath, and put her hand to the door.

"We're assuming he's in the Hall with the rest of the family?" Oliver asked.

Good point. Deanna put her ear to the heavy oak door. Nothing. She knocked once, softly. Then again, louder. She took another breath. She pushed the door open fast lest she think better of it.

The room was empty. Not only no wizard, but none of the wizardly apparatus Deanna had anticipated. No furniture, for that matter. Totally bare. Nothing. The walls were pure white, the stone floor was white, the ceiling—high as all the castle ceilings were high, but not so high as to be in shadow—the ceiling was white. There was no other door, no staircase leading away. They could see the orange blaze of the setting sun through the window, the only glassed-in window she had seen in the castle, whose other casements were protected against the weather by wooden shutters.

"This must be the wrong room," Deanna mused, though there was only one tower, and they were in it, and all the long spiraling flight up, there had been no other doors.

When Oliver didn't answer, she glanced at him. He had taken a step away, so that his back was against the wall opposite the landing from the door. He had his teeth bared.

"Oliver?" she said, remembering what had happened the last time she had ignored his instincts. He looked at her. *Scared,* she realized. "What's the matter?"

"Don't you feel it? The same as by the well. The same as in the courtyard when you acted so strangely with the wizard."

Magic. That was what he was saying. He felt magic in the air. She glanced at the room but there was nothing there. Just an empty room. A clean, well-lighted, empty room.

In a slightly dingy, dark, crowded castle.

And where was all that light coming from, with the sun setting and no candles?

That thought set cold fingers dancing on her back and arms.

But she had come here for a purpose: to retrieve her watch. She had been expecting something wizardly. Just because it manifested itself in the form of an empty white room was no reason to get all goose-bumpy.

She stepped inside. Was it cooler this side of the doorway, or was that just her imagination? She took another step. Something brushed her leg. She jumped with a startled squeak. Nothing there. She yanked her gown up to her knees and brushed at her right calf, where she had felt the spidery touch. She shook the skirt in case anything had gotten up in there.

Oliver hadn't moved away from the far wall. But he had his head tipped as though listening, and he was sniffing the air.

Deanna paused to listen and heard nothing. She sniffed, too. Incense, maybe. A slight mustiness. She took another step toward the window, and her foot came down on something she couldn't see.

Something that jerked out from under her with a shrill cry like a peacock's.

She jumped backward, hitting her hip. Glass crashed as though she had upset a table. The unseen creature she had stepped on cried out again while some bodiless thing in the corner gibbered and hooted and screeched. Perhaps she was safe from that one, for there was a rattling sound also, as though whatever it was shook the bars of a cage.

Cold fingers, or at least they felt like cold fingers, wrapped themselves around her ankle. Deanna screamed. She tried to pull away, kicking with her other foot at whatever it was that held her. The room was still white and well lit and empty, but great flapping wings swooped near her face, tangling in her hair just long enough to make her lose her balance. She fell, still kicking at the thing which gurgled and licked at her ankle.

Her flailing hands knocked over more glass. A smell like chlorine bleach tickled her nostrils. Spilled liquid dripped audibly near her head, sizzling ominously, though there was no visible damage to the white floor. She swung her leg around toward that sound, and whatever had hold of her ankle hissed and let go.

Hands grabbed her wrists. She tensed to break away, then realized it was Oliver. He dragged her to her feet.

Her hands came close to something hot, but she ignored that, as she ignored the invisible glass crunching underfoot while Oliver pulled her toward the door.

Suddenly he pitched forward, letting go of her so as not to yank her down with him. He fell to one knee, brushing away at something which—judging from his expression—must be disgustingly sticky.

This time she pulled him to his feet. She got him through the doorway and pulled the door closed behind them.

They both dropped to their knees in exhaustion on the landing. They had their arms around each other and this time she wasn't embarrassed at all.

"Do you think he'll notice someone's been in there?" she asked once she caught her breath.

Oliver gave her a look which indicated cats—even former cats—didn't recognize sarcasm when they heard it.

She thought of how scared he had looked, refusing to come into the room, and how despite that he *had* come in when she had been in danger. She gave him a little hug, then stood, brushing herself off. "Never mind. We won't go back in there again in a hurry."

"Good," he said.

When they returned to the corridor where their rooms were, they almost stepped into a linen-covered tray which someone had left outside Oliver's door. Farther down the hall, Deanna spotted a similar offering by her door.

So, someone had brought them dinner. No telling who it had been. No telling, either, whether that someone had knocked on their doors and realized that they weren't in.

"Hungry?" she asked Oliver.

He shook his head. His face still had no color in it. She brought his tray into his room anyway, then fetched hers. She plunked herself down on his bed, her legs crossed under her long full skirt, with her tray on her lap.

"Let's see. Pigeon . . ." Her Aunt Emilienne had prepared that when Deanna and her mother had first arrived, so she recognized it. ". . . stuffed with . . . pork, I think . . . mushrooms . . . fresh bread . . . some sort of apple compote . . ." She patted the bed next to her. "You've got to eat, Oliver."

He looked like someone who's remembering the taste of vomiting.

"Oliver, apparently this new body of yours can't handle—" She fought off a wave of nausea of her own.

"—what you're used to eating. But you can't just stop eating all the while we're here." She peered into the pitcher. "Milk!" She sniffed. "Or cream." Definitely not two percent.

At least that got his attention.

She motioned again for him to sit and this time he warily lowered himself next to her. She poured the milk into each of their goblets.

"Cheers," she said, which sophisticated people on TV said, and tapped his goblet with hers.

He watched her drink, then raised his cup, two-handed, to his mouth. For a moment he came close to choking, but then he managed nicely.

She patted his leg encouragingly. "How about some meat?" She cut a piece and held it out on the end of the knife. One thing she had seen at lunch in the Great Hall was that she didn't have to worry about teaching Oliver fastidious table manners—these medieval people used knives, but no forks. The only spoons she had seen had been the ones on Lady Marguerite's nightstand.

Oliver nibbled on the pigeon.

"How is it?"

He nodded and took another bite.

And so it went. He hated carrots, but ate two or three mushrooms. Once she dunked the bread in milk, and he liked that. The apple he admitted was interesting, but he only took one bite. He spat out the wine, which she asked him not to do again, no matter what, and by then he was leaning against her shoulder, his eyes drooping heavily.

"I'll put the tray here, and if you get hungry later

on, the stuff should be just as good cold." But by the time she set the tray by the window and turned back to him, he was curled up, asleep already.

She was used to people taking care of her. How had she ended up being responsible for somebody else? There was some sort of fur skin folded at the foot of the bed—wolf? she wondered—which she took to be the medieval equivalent of a comforter. She tucked it up around Oliver, then carried her tray back to her room.

10 / Octavia

Deanna took one step into her room, then stopped with a sigh.

She look down. She sighed yet again.

She had put her right foot down into a huge bowl of blueberries someone—someone? Leonard, who else?—had left for her. Crushed blueberries oozed over the top of her castle slipper. Thick purple juice soaked through the fabric along the length of her foot, sticking her toes together.

Deanna lifted her leg. The foot came clear of the bowl with a rude, sucking noise. She watched as pieces of fruit slid off the slipper and plopped back into the bowl. "Thank you, Leonard," she muttered to herself. "You shouldn't have." She took off the slipper and hopped across the room to the table with the water pitcher, dripping a purple trail.

She cleaned her foot, and the slipper, as best she could, then set the slipper on the windowsill to dry.

It was beginning to get dark out there, the day almost gone, and she'd accomplished nothing. She stared across the way at the wall that surrounded the castle, protecting its inhabitants. Protecting her, for this one more night. Tomorrow . . . tomorrow was a different matter.

Deanna was angry. Angry with herself for being unable to think what to do, angry with Oliver—who'd been sent to help her and was too busy flirting with Lady Marguerite and learning swordsmanship and getting sick to even be here with her, angry with Leonard and his gifts, angry with the elves, angry with the castle wall, angry with the words the ivy formed on the wall, angry with—

Deanna stopped in the middle of turning from the window.

Angry with the words the ivy formed on the wall?

She took a step away from the window, but only one. Behind her, the setting sun cast an orange glow across the treetops. Slowly she turned back to the window. The vines *had* formed a pattern on the wall, and they were words.

What the ivy said was: *Talk to the pigman, dumb twit of a human girl.*

Oh no, she thought. If the fair folk had known all along, why hadn't they told her to begin with? With a groan of exasperation she put the cold, wet slipper back on and tore out of the room. And almost collided with the wizard.

"Good evening, Lady Deanna," he said, fingering her watch, which hung by a chain around his neck. "Looking for this?"

Deanna took a quick step back. "No," she said, remembering to avoid Algernon's eyes. He seemed to have no power over her if she just remembered to avoid his eyes. And, anyway, her gaze was stuck on her watch, dangling by its buckle on the wizard's chest. "Not at all. What is it?"

He leaned close. Close enough that she could see Mickey Mouse's red shorts. Close enough that Algernon's breath lifted a stray wisp of hair from her cheek. "Something very exciting," he purred. "Something more exciting than anything in my tower room."

Startled to find her intrusion had been discovered so quickly, Deanna looked up. She backed away, and saw the gleam of triumph on Algernon's face.

"Are you and your inhuman companion willing to bargain, Lady Deanna? Are you willing to talk about it?"

Bargain? She turned and ran. Her heart beat so loudly she couldn't hear if footsteps followed. "Oliver!" she cried, bursting into his room. She slammed the door shut behind her and leaned against it.

Oliver had jumped up from the bed, instantly awake and alert. "What's wrong?"

"He's got it," she said, grabbing his arm and shaking him. "Algernon's got the watch."

"Well," Oliver said, relaxing visibly, "you said all along that he would, so it shouldn't come as a surprise."

She came close to strangling him. If she'd thought there was time for it, she might have. "Are you well enough—"

He interrupted: "Why is one of your shoes purple?"

Of all the ridiculous things . . . Still she knew if she

didn't explain, she'd never have his full attention. "I accidentally stepped into a bowl of blueberries and couldn't get the stain out. But that—"

"But it's purple, not blue."

"That's the color of blueberry juice. Listen—"

"Then why aren't they called purpleberries?"

"Oliver!" she screamed at him.

He waited patiently.

"The fair folk left us a message to talk to the pigman."

"All right," he said in a calm, infuriating, let's-not-get-hysterical tone. "Then let's talk to the pigman."

Gingerly she opened the door and peeked up and down the hall. No sign of Algernon. That was little relief. If he wasn't here, where was he? And wherever he was, what was he up to? She motioned for Oliver to follow quietly. Silly. Oliver was always quiet. Her slipper, however, squished noisily with every step.

No one seemed to hear, or at least no one stopped them as they passed through the castle halls and left the main building. They found the pigman, appropriately enough, by the pigpen. He was sitting on the railing, his feet up as though he were on a chaise longue. The pigs were settling down for the night while he blew onto a blade of grass in his cupped hands. The resulting sound was music, soft and fluttery. The resulting sound was, in fact, a lullaby.

One of the pigs grunted, and—as though it had announced their approach—the dusty little man looked over his shoulder and saw them. Immediately he was down from the railing, and the shapeless cap was off his head. "Miss," he mumbled.

Deanna curtsied, because she had curtsied every other time and it seemed rude to stop now. "Sir," she said, "the wizard Algernon has something—"

The pigman hit himself on the side of the head with his cap, causing enough dust to make Deanna cough. "I knew it," he cried. "I knew it wor yours."

"I beg your pardon?"

"That thing. That silver and leather thing what Octavia found."

Deanna glanced at Oliver and couldn't tell what he was thinking. "Octavia?" she repeated. "Who's Octavia?"

"Octavia. The porker what you ate tonight."

Deanna gulped, never having been on a first-name basis with her supper before.

"Where did Octavia find it?" Oliver asked, less sentimental about such things and therefore more practical.

"Well, I like to take the pigs out to the forest sometimes. Give 'em a chance to forage. Something different. Anyway, there's this pool there. Said to be enchanted, but I never seen anything enchanted there. This morning I brung the pigs there and Octavia, she just stuck her snout into the edge of the water and pulled that thing up outta the mud and shook it like this." He made a motion like a dog worrying a slipper. "That wor right before you come, miss. I kept trying to ask, but never seemed to get the chance."

Guiltily, Deanna remembered holding her breath and ignoring him. "So how did Algernon get it from you?"

"I give it to him, miss. Just now."

"You gave it to him?" But then she thought back to the courtyard, how the wizard's eyes had gotten all whirly and her free will had seemed to melt away. She would have given the watch to Algernon too, under those circumstances, and never have thought to miss it.

"Did I do something wrong, miss?" the pigman asked. "I'm terrible sorry if I did. Terrible sorry."

"That's all right," she said, more to make him feel better than because she really believed it. "I'll get it back."

"Yes, miss. He'll give it to you, miss, if you explain it be yorn."

She sighed but didn't argue. "Thank you. Come on, Oliver."

"Miss," the pigman called after them. "I hope you get your magic back."

She was about to call back that she didn't have any magic and never had, but decided that was something she probably shouldn't yell across the courtyard.

No telling who might hear.

11 / Plans

"Oliver, what are we going to do?" Deanna asked as they walked back toward the castle.

Oliver shook his head, with his best don't-ask-me-you're-in-charge look. "I'll do whatever you want me to do," he said.

She had no answer for him either.

They rounded a corner and saw Leonard standing on the lawn, facing the castle. And singing. He had accompaniment: bored-looking servants playing lute, harp, cymbals, and something that looked like a clarinet but sounded like the moan of a humpback whale. He sang, loudly and off-key: "My love is like a cold, cold frost. . . . But when I die, she will feel lost . . ."

A dog started to bark, then another, then several. A rooster crowed. Those servants who had to be up earliest and so went to bed earliest banged on the shutters and yelled for quiet. Leonard got louder, to be heard over the racket, and gazed up at what had to be Deanna's bedroom window with a sick-puppy expression.

Her legs got quivery and she sat down heavily on the ground.

"Deanna?" Oliver sounded worried. He crouched down beside her, but she didn't want to look at him. She crossed her legs Indian style and hunched over in the evening gloom, her arms hugged around herself. Without touching her, without knowing anything of human comforting, he said, "Maybe something you ate?"

Her life was going to end here, she thought, in a place even less familiar than the Guyon farmhouse, surrounded by strangers who were getting stranger all the time. She had been gone all day, which would have her mother in a panic; her only confidant was a cat; and her only plan for dealing with the impossible task she had been set had been to cross her fingers and hope that things would work out. Well, things hadn't worked out, and by noon tomorrow there wouldn't even be anybody left to miss her.

"What should I *do?*" she whispered into the lengthening shadows, as though the fair folk could hear her. It wasn't a matter of being unwilling; she couldn't begin to guess where to begin.

Leonard's voice warbled, "My love has eyes of wondrous brown. . . . Pray, don't look upon my song and frown . . ."

Deanna rocked back and forth, wondering if it would hurt to die or if she would just suddenly cease to exist, gone like the flame on a birthday candle.

Oliver watched her silently, still close enough to touch. Still not touching.

A voice behind her announced, "Somebody should do something."

Deanna jumped.

It was Baylen standing there in the almost-dark; and when she continued to sit there, looking at him with her jaw hanging loose, he nodded toward his brother and said, "Leonard. Somebody should do something to get him to stop."

"Oh," Deanna said, for it had seemed for a moment as though he'd been reading her thoughts. "Leonard."

Baylen looked at her as though she were a mildly distasteful idiot. He raised his eyebrows at Oliver, gave her a hint of a bow, and started to leave.

"Baylen," she called after him. "Help me."

Baylen paused, his expression quizzical. "With Leonard?"

"With my quest."

The flicker of interest dissolved into disappointment.

But she remembered how Baylen had rescued her, all unwittingly, by interrupting Algernon when he'd tried his mind-control spells in the courtyard. She scrambled to her feet. "Please, Baylen. I don't have anybody else to turn to."

Silently, with a graceful uncurling motion, Oliver stood.

Lamely, she added, "Oliver and I don't have anybody else to turn to."

"Why don't I get my Uncle Algernon?" Baylen suggested. "He's good at that sort of—"

"No!" she cried. She glanced over her shoulder to make sure she hadn't attracted Leonard's attention. "No," she repeated more calmly. "Not Algernon."

Baylen was interested again. He came closer. "Don't tell me Uncle Algernon is competing with Leonard for your attention."

"No," she said. Then, deciding she would get nowhere if she didn't trust *some*one, she told him: "Your uncle has the thing I need—the object of my quest."

"Ah!" Baylen stroked his chin. "Then why don't you ask him for it?"

"He wouldn't give it to me. I know he wouldn't. Baylen, we need some sort of plan, and Oliver and I can't come up with one."

"Well . . ." Baylen said. She had agonized over telling him, and here he was looking bored and obviously trying to think of a way to get out of becoming involved.

Beyond them, Leonard started a new song, one that proclaimed his love was fairer than any other's.

Instantly Baylen shifted from bemused to annoyed. Deanna had taken the song as a tribute to her rather than a comment on Baylen's betrothed, but apparently the older brother saw Leonard's wording as a personal affront. His gaze slipped from her to Leonard back to her.

Sorry, I can't help you; I'll be beating up my brother, she thought he was about to say. Or some such thing. Instead, he said, "Let's talk someplace else. Away from . . ." He glanced away in Leonard's direction once more.

It was too good to be true, and who cared what his reasoning was? "Oh, Baylen," she said. "Thank you." She glanced at Oliver, to share her relief with him.

If he was relieved, he did a fine job of hiding it.

What was the matter now? Was Oliver's sulky expression because she had said she had no one to turn to? There was no time to ask, for Baylen was pulling on her arm, leading her away from his brother and his songs.

At least Oliver followed without objection. Baylen led them to the mews, where the hunting birds were kept. The place stank of the sputtering torch Baylen lit, and of leather and bird droppings, but at least they were alone. In the silence, Deanna could hear the hawks—or eagles or falcons or whatever they were—shift nervously from one foot to the other, jingling the tiny bells attached to the little hoods that covered their eyes. Oliver looked inordinately interested in the birds, so Deanna plunged into her story as soon as Baylen faced her. "This object of mine," she said, "it's called a watch."

"*Watch?*" Baylen repeated. "Like a guard goes on watch?"

Good grief. If people started thinking it had some military significance, she'd never get it back. "No, nothing like that. It's the little thing your uncle got from the pigman this evening. He's wearing it around his neck. It doesn't do anything. It's just called a watch because it . . . it's pretty to watch."

That was stupid, and she knew it was stupid even as she said it.

Baylen looked at her levelly and said, "That doesn't sound like something Uncle Algernon would be interested in at all."

"Well, the thing is, he doesn't know that it doesn't do anything."

"Ah. What does he *think* it does?"

"I . . . don't know," Deanna admitted.

Baylen chewed on his lip, apparently thinking a lot faster than he was talking. "Hmm. All right. I know how to get it. I'll tell him I've found out what it can do, that I overheard you and Oliver talking and that it . . . Let's see . . ." Even in the failing light she could see the sparkle in his eyes when the idea came to him. "I'll tell him it's something for use in alchemy: for changing lead to gold."

Deanna glanced at Oliver to see if this made any more sense to him than it did to her, but she couldn't tell what he was thinking. She said, "Yes, but Baylen, that'll only make him want the watch even more. We have to make him think it's something he doesn't want, maybe that it's dangerous to him."

"No!" Baylen said. "No, no, no, no. You don't understand this type of subterfuge at all. If Uncle Algernon thought it was dangerous, he'd never let it out of his sight. I'll tell him it's something nice and safe, and then he won't be so careful with it."

Baylen was right about one thing: she certainly didn't know anything about subterfuge. But she supposed it made a sort of sense as he explained it. "But if he thinks it'll make gold, won't he want to make gold with it?"

"Yes," Baylen said. "How not? But we'll tell him—I'll tell him—that the magic of the watch only works . . . if no one is watching it."

Deanna concentrated, trying to imagine Algernon believing this. She couldn't.

"No. It's coming to me. It's called a watch because it alone must watch over the alchemic process. The watch . . . Let's see . . . The watch must be placed at a crossroads where a man has been hanged from a gallows." Baylen ignored the face Deanna made and continued: "This must be done at midnight, by the light—oh, this is good!—by the light of the first full moon after the winter solstice."

Winter solstice? That didn't sound promising, considering it was August. "When's the winter solstice?" she asked.

Baylen gave her a look which indicated anyone with any sense at all knew when the winter solstice was.

"December twenty-second," Oliver answered. Then, just as smoothly: "Is that soon?"

Baylen tapped his head in the same *nothing upstairs* gesture that Deanna knew from nine hundred years later in Greeley, Colorado.

"Baylen," she said. "Baylen, listen to me. This is important."

"What?"

"This has to be done tonight."

"Tonight?" Baylen frowned. He looked bitterly disappointed. "How about by the light of any full moon?"

"Is there one tonight?"

"No."

"Baylen, forget the moon. I'm perfectly serious about this: I must have that watch and I must be back in the forest by midday tomorrow. At. The. Latest."

Baylen tugged on his mustache. "Can we keep the crossroads with the gallows?"

She considered. He seemed to be making all of this more complicated than it needed to be. "Only if there's one nearby," she told him.

He sighed. "Eight or nine furlongs."

"What's a furlong?"

"Two-oh-one point one-six-eight meters," Oliver explained.

It was Deanna's turn to sigh. "I was never good at metric."

"About an eighth of a mile."

Times eight or nine . . . So, a bit over a mile all told; about a twenty-minute walk. "That's not bad."

Baylen was looking from Oliver to Deanna. "What's a mile?" he asked.

"Eight furlongs," Oliver said. He tapped his head.

Baylen showed his teeth in a grin that was unsettlingly similar to Algernon's.

Was all this really going to get her watch back? "So, at the crossroads . . ." Deanna prompted.

"At the crossroads," Baylen continued, "at midnight. It must be placed in a box of oak, and the box must be placed in an iron cauldron. One gold coin goes at the bottom of the cauldron, then the whole thing is filled with base metals of any sort—broken blades, rusted armor, scrap tin. The box, with the watch inside it, rests on top." He paused, thinking.

"Go on," Deanna urged.

"Once the box has been set in place, no one must look at it. Which is why the watch is called a watch:

because it alone will watch over the alchemic process." Baylen was obviously pleased with that touch. He intoned: "Let no human eye behold the cauldron between the rising of the moon and the coming of the sun, or the spell will be reversed and the gold . . ." He paused for dramatic effect. ". . . lost."

Deanna considered. It was reasonable. Sort of. She guessed. Perhaps Algernon would be greedy enough to risk having the watch out of sight for a few short hours. She glanced at Oliver, who looked skeptical.

"Trust me," Baylen said. And, after all, what other choice had she?

"Tonight," she reminded him.

"Tonight," he assured her.

12 / Night

You go back to your room," Baylen told her, "while I set things up with Uncle Algernon."

Deanna hesitated. Oliver just stood there with his arms folded and she couldn't even tell for sure if he was looking at Baylen or beyond him at the roosting birds.

Baylen said, "If he sees us together, that would spoil everything; then he'd never believe our story."

Deanna could see the logic of it, and yet she had the sense that something was wrong, if she could just figure out what. Things were moving too fast. *Our* story was it now?

Baylen sighed impatiently. "And you can't wait here: somebody is sure to notice the torchlight and come investigating to see who's here at this hour."

"All right," said Deanna. The alternative was to remain in the mews in the dark, inhaling the bird stink and hoping that Oliver wasn't thinking about the falcons as an after-dinner snack. "Come on, Oliver."

She and Oliver crossed the darkened courtyard, and thank goodness Leonard had apparently given up on her. There was no sign of him or his musical entourage on the lawn. The huge doors to the castle were open, spilling golden torchlight out onto the entryway.

"Now," Deanna said as they slipped inside, "if we can just avoid Leonard and Algernon . . ."

She knew she shouldn't have said it. A statement like that was just inviting bad luck. As soon as the words were out of her mouth, she regretted it, even before she heard a footstep on the stone floor behind them. She whirled around, crying, "What do you want from me?" which was an appropriate question for either Leonard or Algernon.

But not for Sir Henri, who took two steps back and stammered, "Ah, well, ahm, ah, nothing."

"I'm sorry," Deanna said. "I thought you were . . ." Your son? Your brother? She couldn't very well say either. "You startled me," she finished lamely. Obviously he could have said the same to her. "Forgive me."

Sir Henri bowed, ever gracious. "Nothing to forgive, my dear. But there's nothing here at Belesse that should give you such a start. Nothing and nobody dangerous about the place at all."

She could have said, *Yeah? Have you been in your brother's room lately?* But she didn't.

In the second she lost thinking it, Sir Henri's attention went to Oliver. "Feeling better, my boy?"

"Than what?" Oliver asked.

Deanna dug her elbow into his side. "Yes, he is." She smiled and nodded.

Oliver imitated the gesture, watching her while he did.

"Much better," Deanna said.

"Much," Oliver agreed.

"Good," Sir Henri said. "Excellent. Poor Marguerite didn't feel well at dinner either."

"What did she eat?" Oliver asked, but Deanna gave him another good hard nudge in the ribs.

Sir Henri didn't seem to notice. "She got one of her sick headaches and had to leave supper and go to bed early. It happened quite suddenly. Right in the middle of Baylen telling how he won last year's tournament at Whitney Castle." He scratched his head as a thought occurred. "Strange. She's heard Baylen tell the story at least a dozen times and she's never gotten a headache before."

"Oh well," Deanna said. "You never can tell."

"I suppose not," Sir Henri agreed. "Good night." He started down the corridor but then turned back. "By the way, you haven't seen Baylen recently, have you? Or Leonard?"

"Recently?" Deanna repeated. "Not *real* recently." It had been . . . what? At least two minutes.

"Hmm," their father said. "It's just that sometimes, left alone, the two of them can get into trouble."

"Perhaps Leonard's in the garden," Oliver suggested. He turned to Deanna. "He did seem fond of the garden that one time."

"What one time?" Deanna asked.

"When the two of you went there together and he was rolling around in the grass under the wooden bench."

Maybe she'd get lucky and the earth would open up and swallow her.

"Well," Sir Henri said, "they're sure to turn up eventually. Nobody disappears forever. Good night."

Deanna waved. As soon as he was out of sight she muttered, "It's eleven o'clock: Do you know where your children are?"

"I have no children," Oliver explained patiently.

"Oh, Oliver. What am I going to do with you?"

She had noticed, however, that he hadn't asked about Lady Marguerite's condition or indicated any concern. Neither had he suggested that they go to her room to make sure she was all right. Deanna didn't know if that made her feel better or worse, that Oliver showed no more loyalty to Lady Marguerite than to Deanna herself. Wasn't that just like a cat? she asked herself.

They waited for Baylen in her room.

This high up in the castle the window openings were much wider than those closer to the ground, so she sat on the windowsill and asked Oliver to sit with her. She hoped that if Leonard was out there, watching in the dark, he'd become discouraged, seeing Oliver with her.

Deanna sat with her knees drawn up to her chin, thinking. What she was thinking was that the fair folk were idiots for not getting to her sooner with the message about the pigman. But it was her world, her life on the line, not theirs. And, in all fairness, there was no telling how long the ivy on the wall had been exhorting her to action before she'd noticed it. She couldn't, in good conscience, blame it entirely on them.

She sighed. She wasn't supposed to be trying to

find someone to blame this situation on; she was supposed to be trying to find a way out of it.

Facing her on the ledge, Oliver was in much the same pose as she, chin resting on knee, arms circling legs. As always he was wearing his long-sleeved shirt and the fur vest; despite the August heat, he always seemed to feel cold. In the flickering candlelight, she could see that his face had gotten the beginnings of a sunburn, just from being out this afternoon. It was as though his fair skin had never seen the sun, she thought—before she remembered. The color was very becoming, she had to admit to herself—even if he had failed her this afternoon by going off with Baylen and Sir Henri.

Deanna became aware that all the while she had been thinking, Oliver was watching her with those eyes which were so pretty in a cat but disturbing in a young man. Back home, sometimes, Deanna had been afraid that there wasn't as much to her as there was to other people, that her emotions were too near the surface and that she missed the undercurrents of life. It had nothing to do with intelligence, but with feelings, and what she felt, occasionally, was that she didn't have as many as other people, that she was without substance and merely role-playing at life. Now, looking at Oliver, at those big green eyes that seemed to be constantly evaluating, she feared she was a disappointment to him as well as to herself.

"What are you thinking?" she asked.

He shook his head, apparently unwilling to share. Or perhaps he wasn't thinking at all. Perhaps it was no more than the same thoughtful expression of any cat sitting in any window. She didn't believe that for a moment.

She looked away from him, into the darkness outside. Where was Baylen? His plan had better be a good one, for there'd be little time left for second tries. Eventually—*eventually?* How late was it? Eleven-thirty, twelve o'clock in the normal world? Deanna had never realized before how used she was to being able to glance at her wrist or a nearby wall to check the passing of time—eventually she saw Baylen crossing the lawn. He stood below the window and beckoned. Her anxious anticipation turned to a more quiet desperation.

Starting. It was finally starting.

"All set?" she asked Oliver.

He slid off the windowsill without a word.

They made it only as far as the hall outside her bedroom door. "My hat," she said. Once they were gone, that might turn back into her ponytail fastener and who knew what the people here would make of that? She stopped with her hand to the door and turned to Oliver. "Is there anything you . . ."

She suddenly felt as though all the air had been knocked out of her. Oliver didn't have any things from the twentieth century. He had only what the fair folk had given him: the sword, the clothes he was wearing. His humanity. Things which would disappear upon their return to the real world. Deanna had known that all along. She just hadn't thought about it before.

And she'd never have guessed how much it would hurt.

"I have everything I brought," Oliver said, his voice, as ever, giving her no hint to his thoughts.

They had bickered and snarled and snapped at each other and she had never anticipated missing him, but there it was. *He's just a cat,* she thought. She'd thought it before. No use making things any worse than they were. Any regrets, any sadness would be on her part only. Wouldn't they?

She didn't ask, and he didn't say. He waited outside her room while she fastened the hat securely. She looked down at her slippers, one palest lilac, one blueberry-stained. (Purpleberry *did* make more sense.) *Still . . . ,* she thought, and sighed.

Outside it had gotten quite dark. Deanna wouldn't have been able to see anything if there hadn't been torches placed in sconces every several hundred feet the entire inside length of the wall that surrounded Castle Belesse. The nights here seemed clearer but much blacker than the nights in Greeley or Chalon, where the city lights always cast up into the sky, obliterating stars but giving a gray glow overhead. Somehow, despite the additional stars visible this way, the night felt more forbidding, more likely to close in on them.

A figure jumped out of the shadows at her.

Deanna gasped, too startled to scream.

The shadow creature kissed her hand. "Go, go," he commanded, waving an arm at other shadows behind him.

Music started, like the moan of a humpback whale.

"Leonard!" Deanna was shaking, unable to pull her hand away. "Are you trying to kill me with a heart attack or what?"

Leonard waved impatiently at another clump of shadow.

"Hey, hey, up! One, two, three, over!" Tumblers sprinted, somersaulted, cartwheeled out of the darkness. "Hey, ho, ooop-la!" They jumped on each other's shoulders, then leapt or somersaulted off. One rolled like a tumbleweed, weaving in and out among Deanna, Oliver, and Leonard. Another did a high jump between Deanna and Leonard, over their still-clasped hands. "Yip, yip, ha!"

Deanna felt like a stage prop as the acrobats dived and cavorted among them. Oliver wasn't helping. He looked as though he was enjoying the show. "Leonard," she shouted over the noise of the performers, "Leonard—"

"My love is like a cold, cold frost," Leonard warbled.

"Leonard." It was Baylen who stepped out of the shadows this time. "Leonard, that's enough now."

Leonard raised his hand and made a slashing gesture. The music stopped as abruptly as lifting a needle from a record. The tumblers ceased half a heartbeat later, with the exception of one man who was hanging by his knees from his fellows' extended arms and had obviously missed the signal. He flipped over, where there was nobody to check his momentum, and he landed on his back with a muffled "Umph."

"Sorry, my lady." Baylen kissed her hand. "Leonard had this little performance planned, and I had to agree to it in order to get his promise that he'd help us with our little plan." He wiggled his eyebrows conspiratorially at her.

Leonard shooed the servants away, then dropped to his knees and began kissing her hand. "Ah, fairest desiring of my heart," he murmured between kisses, "you have no idea how happy you've made me."

Deanna was having trouble remembering how to breathe. She'd been wrong: she wasn't going to die of a heart attack, she was going to die of embarrassment. In front of Oliver, no less. "What—" She was panting, watching the tumblers leave, afraid they'd come back and start up again. "—help?"

"See," Baylen said to Leonard. "You've got her so upset, she can't even remember the plan."

In a perfectly un-upset voice, Oliver repeated her question: "What help?"

Baylen cast him a dirty look, a watch-out-or-you'll-spoil-everything look. He spoke between clenched teeth, his tone saying, *I'm not used to dealing with fools.* "Help getting Lady Deanna's watch back from Uncle Algernon, of course," he said. "Since it can turn lead to gold, she needs it back."

Deanna looked from Baylen to Leonard. What was going on? Baylen had never said anything about getting help from Leonard. And if Leonard was going to help them, why hadn't Baylen told him that the lead-to-gold story was only for Algernon's benefit?

"Trust me, my lady," Baylen said. "I'll get your watch back for you."

"*I'll* get your watch," Leonard protested smoothly.

"*We'll* get your watch," Baylen corrected even more smoothly.

She tried to swallow down the lump in her throat.

"Deanna?" Oliver said.

But it was too late to call things off, if Algernon had already been convinced to place the watch at the crossroads.

"Oh," she said. "*That* help."

Baylen grinned, his teeth gleaming in the light of the torches. "This is going to be so much fun," he said.

13 / Complications

"We'd better get started," Baylen said.

All the questions Deanna had to ask him, and she couldn't ask any. There was no telling how much Leonard knew, or how much Leonard knew that she knew, or how much he guessed . . . Her head was beginning to spin again. Presumably Algernon had believed Baylen's story about the watch having the power to change lead to gold. That much she was fairly certain of, or why would there be any need to get started at all? But if Baylen had changed the plan by including—sort of—Leonard, she couldn't be certain what he had told Algernon either. *Idiot,* she scolded herself for ever asking Baylen for help. But she said nothing and only kept alert for some sign of his intentions as Baylen led them out through the gate of the castle wall and over the moat and across a field.

However, Leonard rose to the occasion. "All right," he demanded. "So what's this so-called plan of yours?"

Baylen made an expansive gesture. "Deanna's watch."

"What about it?"

"She entrusted me with the secret meaning behind it."

"So what?" Leonard said. "She entrusted all of us."

"Yes, but she told *me* first."

"Did not."

"Did too."

"Did not."

"Did too."

With a smirk, Leonard pointed out: "Obviously she told Oliver first."

"Oh yeah?" Baylen stopped, scowling, while he tried to come up with a better answer. "Oh yeah?"

Deanna stamped her foot. "Baylen! Leonard!"

"Anyway," Baylen lied, "she told *me* what ingredients this alchemy spell needs for the watch to work, and she entrusted me to gather those materials."

"So how come you came crawling to me for help?" Leonard sneered.

Deanna could read Baylen's emotional struggle on his face: the conflicting desires to prove his superiority to Leonard or to pacify him so that he would help. "Well," Baylen admitted, "there was one thing I couldn't get, which I knew you could."

Amazing. What was going on?

Leonard beamed at her. "See? Helpless without me. Pray tell me, Baylen—" He made a sweeping bow. "—how can I help you?"

Don't overdo it, Deanna thought, estimating that Baylen would make him pay later for each squirm he caused now.

Baylen said, "One thing I couldn't get. Uncle Algernon is waiting at the gallows crossroads for the final ingredient which we're hoping you can get."

"Which is?"

"Seawater."

"Seawater?" Leonard said.

"Seawater?" Deanna said.

"Seawater," Baylen said.

Oh, good grief. They weren't anywhere near the sea.

"Now you might be thinking that we aren't anywhere near the sea," Baylen said.

"No," Leonard proclaimed in sarcastic disbelief that Deanna mentally echoed.

"But we are closer than you think."

Oliver looked at Deanna with raised eyebrows. *How did I let myself get talked into this?* she asked herself. Couldn't Baylen have come up with something more sensible?

"There is an underground stream," Baylen told them, "that leads from the sea to the pond in serf Guillaume's holding."

"The pond has seawater?" Leonard asked incredulously.

"You see, that was the problem—"

"The pond has seawater?" Leonard interrupted.

"—Lady Deanna knew that she needed seawater, but didn't know where to get any near here—"

"The pond has *seawater?"* Leonard persisted.

"Will you shut up and let me finish?"

Between clenched teeth, Leonard said, "There is no such thing as a stream, underground or not, leading from the sea to Guillaume's pond."

"Uncle Algernon found it," Baylen said smugly.

"How?"

"Uncle Algernon has his ways."

"Hmmm." Apparently that wasn't something Leonard was going to argue with. He looked at Deanna, who looked at Oliver, who looked as though everything they were saying was perfectly reasonable. Leonard snorted. "So we get some water from the pond. So what?"

"No, no, no, no," Baylen said in that condescending way that set Deanna's teeth on edge. "We don't get some water from the pond. We get some water from the stream."

"So," Leonard repeated, *"what?"*

"It's an underground stream. You need to go to the mouth of the stream, at the bottom of the pond."

"Ah," Leonard said. "That's one deep pond."

"That's why we need you," Baylen told him. "You're the best swimmer in the family."

"Yes, I am, though I'm surprised you finally admit it. But how will I know where this seawater comes in?"

"Uncle Algernon says it's in the middle of the pond. He says the water's warmer there. You'll be able to tell."

"I don't know," Leonard said thoughtfully.

"Please, Leonard," Deanna begged, for although she resented getting caught up in Baylen's intrigues, obviously he was set on this. "We can't even start unless you say yes."

"Well," Leonard said slowly, basking in all the attention. "All right. Yes."

14 / Alchemy

The pond Baylen had chosen was, of course, in the opposite direction from the crossroads he had chosen. It was about the size and shape of a soccer field and, according to the brothers, about five times as deep as a man was tall. It was surrounded by small cultivated fields belonging to various serfs who owed allegiance to Sir Henri—holdings, Baylen and Leonard called them. Baylen and Leonard had fought with and teased each other all the way there, and Deanna was ready to pull her hair out.

"Well," said Baylen, "we're here."

"Thank you for pointing that out for us," Leonard said, standing at the edge of the pond. "We're so lucky to have an expert with us."

Baylen smirked. "Do you plan on actually entering the water, or do you intend to stand here and tell us how good you're going to be at it?" He held out the stoppered vial Leonard was supposed to fill with sea-water. But then, as though on second thought, he said, "Come to think of it, you'd probably do better to get undressed. You don't want to be walking around in wet clothes for the rest of the night."

Leonard glanced at Deanna.

"You don't mind waiting behind those bushes, do you, Deanna? To spare our Leonard's modesty?"

Deanna shrugged helplessly and went behind the bushes that separated two of the holdings. She sat down wearily and rested her head against her knees. Someone had planted mint among the bushes. The biting scent was so pungent that, had she more energy, Deanna would have moved away. "I can't believe we're doing this," she told Oliver.

He stooped down beside her and asked, "What exactly are we doing?"

Deanna shook her head. "I wish I knew."

They were close enough that she could hear the splash as Leonard entered the water, then the *slap-slap* sound of his swimming out to the center of the pond.

She sat listening to that, and to the crickets, until Baylen came around the bushes and grinned. He held his finger to his lips to caution silence and asked in hushed tones, "Ready to go?"

It was only then that she noticed Leonard's clothes tucked under his arm. "Oh, that's common, Baylen," Deanna snapped. "Common and nasty and juvenile."

Again he made the shushing gesture. "Yes, I'm rather pleased with it myself."

"Baylen—"

"Shh. If he hears you, he'll come out. If he comes out, he'll ruin the plan. If he ruins the plan, you'll never get your watch back."

"But . . ." She couldn't see how abandoning Leonard out in the middle of nowhere without any clothes was going to get her the watch back. This was pure be-rotten-to-Leonard nastiness on Baylen's part.

"Listen, we can call this off now," Baylen offered. "Do you want to do this or not?"

Actually not. But Baylen was her best choice. In the dark, she couldn't even tell where they were, much less how to get to wherever Algernon had left the watch. *If* Baylen had gotten him to leave the watch. *If* Baylen had ever even talked to him about the watch. She had to admit—despite the fact that she hated the trite sound of it—that her fate was in Baylen's hands. Baylen wasn't her best chance, he was her only chance.

Deanna sighed and got to her feet. If she was lucky, she thought, they'd be out of hearing range by the time Leonard discovered he'd been abandoned.

She wasn't lucky.

They were walking across a field planted with some sort of grain—barley, possibly—when his voice caught up with them, hardly more than a whisper of wind in the leaves. "Baylen!" They had covered quite a distance and Leonard must have been shouting with all his might for the sound to reach them at all. She had never done anything so low, she thought. But, after all, what could she do? Baylen had the clothes. What was her alternative? To tackle him, grab Leonard's pants, bring them back to him, and cease to exist by noon?

"Bay-len!"

And Baylen only grinned.

Oliver had glanced at her once, at the first call, as

though to check whether her ears could pick out the sound, but his expression told her nothing.

Deanna set her face—this was none of her business, she told herself—and put one foot ahead of the other. "Bayyyy-lennnn!" she heard again, fainter than before. Perhaps Leonard's voice was giving out, or he was realizing the fruitlessness of it all. And then she thought she heard it one more time, but that may have been a breeze rattling the leaves; and after that they continued to the crossroads in silence. *Baylen's plan better be worth it,* she thought. It'd better have convinced Algernon to leave the watch untended. Otherwise she'd have to face Leonard again, and how could she do that?

She knew they were close when Baylen put his finger to his lips although nobody had said anything since the pond. Silently he pointed to a wooded area, then made a curlicue gesture that she assumed meant they'd circle into the woods and come up onto the crossroads from behind—longer but safer. She nodded.

The woods were dark, with exposed roots to trip her up, and twigs that hung down and snagged in her hair. No telling how many insects were nesting in there by now. The night was hot and humid and her hair and her clothes stuck to her.

There was no path that Deanna could see. Baylen stuffed Leonard's clothes underneath a bush and began to pick his way with a self-assurance that Deanna figured would in no time either get them exactly where he wanted or have them hopelessly lost. She kept turning around to make sure Oliver was still there, because he never made a sound.

Finally, it must have been four o'clock where people had clocks, Baylen turned around to once more place finger to lips. Then he got down on his hands and knees and very, very stealthily crawled forward.

Deanna and Oliver followed, and in a few moments were at the edge of the trees. They had come out in the angle where the two roads intersected, and were maybe a hundred yards away; it was hard for Deanna to judge: perhaps the distance from her front yard to that of her best friend Lynn, two houses away. Two houses, and about nine hundred years. There was no cover at all—nothing to hide behind—just wild grass and weeds between them, crouching at the edge of the woods, and the cauldron, sitting by itself in the middle of the road.

But there was nobody else there. Apparently Algernon had believed the story Baylen had invented about the watch and the gold and the "let no human eye . . ." Apparently.

Deanna squinted into the shadows up and down the lengths of the two roads, same as Baylen and Oliver were doing. Crickets chirped, mosquitoes whined, but nothing out of the ordinary seemed to be stirring tonight. *Don't forget you're stirring,* Deanna told herself. But even with a cynical outlook she could find nothing suspicious in the colorless landscape she surveyed.

Baylen started to get up and Oliver tugged on his sleeve. He pointed to the left, where there were some bushes across the road.

"What?" Baylen asked in a barely audible whisper.

"Someone sitting there," Oliver whispered back.

Deanna and Baylen tried to pick a shape out of the shadows. "I see nothing," Baylen said. Deanna's thought exactly.

"Two men," Oliver described to them. "The one on the right has light curly hair and a sleeveless leather tunic. The other has longer, darker hair and a short-sleeved shirt. I can't make out the color in this light. They have their backs to us and appear to be asleep, although it's hard to say for certain."

It took Baylen a good second to remember to shut his mouth. He glanced from Oliver to the shadows across the road. He gave a low, appreciative whistle and said, "You must have the eyes of a cat."

"Yes," Oliver said.

"If there're two, there may be more," Deanna whispered.

"With instructions *not* to look at the cauldron," Baylen reminded them. "Uncle Algernon believed every word I told him. He thinks he's making gold. He'll have told his people *not* to look at the cauldron. They'll be facing away from us. If they're awake—which they probably won't be. If there's more than the two sleepers to begin with."

Deanna looked at Oliver, who appeared none too pleased by all this. "What is it?" she asked.

He seemed to be listening to the night sounds. He shook his head. "Something's not right."

Baylen sighed impatiently, as though to say, *Amateurs always get cold feet*. "We can't back out now. What would you say to Uncle Algernon?"

What would she say to Leonard? "Surely there has

to be another way," she said. "There's always more than one way to skin a cat."

Oliver looked up sharply.

"Sorry. I meant—"

"This is safe," Baylen interrupted. "My lady, trust me . . . Nothing is wrong. This is just last-moment jitters."

Oliver didn't get last-moment jitters, Deanna was willing to bet. But Baylen was right about one thing: this wouldn't get any easier by postponing it. By tomorrow afternoon she wouldn't even be a memory unless the fair folk were wrong, and she had stopped believing that long ago. "All right. We'll do it," she said, figuring if the situation were that dangerous, Oliver would object.

He didn't.

"All right," Baylen said. "We'll wait a bit to make sure nobody's stirring."

The "bit" stretched out agonizingly. At least an hour of nothing.

The darkness.

The croaking frogs.

The smell of grass.

The sweat drying on her back, prickling like a hundred creepy-crawlers.

She shifted position and tried to ease a cramp out of her leg. Which way was east? Was that the first hint of dawn in the sky?

Finally Baylen asked, "Are the guards still there?"

Oliver nodded.

"Do they still look asleep?"

Again Oliver nodded.

"Then we'll go now. We'll approach together, just in case there is trouble. Deanna, you seize the watch. Oliver, you stand to her left, keeping a special eye on those guards. I'll protect her right."

Deanna's heart was beating harder than it had when she'd been fighting through the underbrush in the woods. Could the others see how scared she was? She hoped not: they both looked so calm.

"Ready?" Baylen asked. "Keep low. Forced-march pace."

What's forced-march pace? Deanna was about to ask, but didn't have the chance. Just short of a run, she saw, panting already to keep up. There was no breeze to cool the hot, sticky air. And Baylen moved them forward in a weaving pattern, which took them three times as long to cover the distance. *Any more excitement and they're going to have to pick me up and carry me,* she thought as they reached the cauldron.

No sign that anyone was watching or aware of them.

With Oliver several paces away to one side, and Baylen several paces away to the other, Deanna turned her attention to the cauldron. It was enormous, big enough that Deanna could easily have fit inside it. *Must have been awful carrying it out here,* she thought. And it was filled, as Baylen had said it should be, with metal of all sorts. Mostly armor, she noted. *This is finally over,* she thought. *Look out, elves, here I come.* The small wooden box was perched at the top. Her hands closed around it, lifted it, removed it from the pile. Mostly armor, but it started to settle, to tip, and oh no, the guards would be sure to hear, except it wasn't settling after all, it was moving upward, and a silvery gauntlet grabbed hold of her wrist, and the gauntlet was attached to an armpiece which was attached to a cuirass, and it was an entire chain-mail-armored man who'd been crouched down in that enormous cauldron with a few stray pieces of scrap metal to camouflage him, but now he had hold of her, and the wooden box had dropped from her fingers which were becoming numb from the pressure of his restraining her, and that was Algernon's face leering at her from underneath that helmet, and a dozen armed guards had jumped out from behind trees and bushes and clumps of dirt that had seemed too small to hide anybody, but now they had their swords and crossbows and pikes leveled at Oliver and Baylen and Deanna, and Algernon said, "Are you ready to talk now?"

15 / "Who's the Leader of the Club...?"

"Uncle Algernon," Baylen said with a nervous laugh, "it's me, Baylen."

Still holding on to her, the wizard looked beyond Deanna to his nephew. "I see who it is, you meddling idiot. Put your hands up."

"Uncle Algernon!" Baylen tried to sound indignant, but the drawn weapons were obviously making him edgy.

"Put your hands up."

Baylen put them up.

Oliver, wearing what Deanna considered his I-told-you-so look, raised his hands also.

"Somebody's going to get hurt, with all those weapons," Baylen grumbled as Algernon motioned two of his men forward.

"Nobody's going to get hurt," Algernon said, never loosening his grip on Deanna.

Ha!

"Now you've done it," she said. "You can kiss your gold good-bye, you know."

Algernon gave her that boy-are-you-a-halfwit look. "Gold?" he said. "Under the moon? Everybody knows gold is aligned with the sun, not the moon."

Everybody?

The men took Baylen's sword and Oliver's, then patted them up and down searching for hidden weapons. Oliver had a knife that Deanna hadn't known of. Resourceful—not that it made any difference now.

Baylen gave a baleful glare at the young man who searched him. "Boy, Norman, you just wait until I tell my father," he snarled. "Are you going to be in trouble."

Norman didn't appear overly daunted by the idea.

With her companions disarmed, Algernon finally released Deanna. He stood looking at her as though she were a minor annoyance, but mostly weighing, evaluating. It was the sort of look Oliver—when he'd still been a cat—had given Aunt Emilienne's goldfish, as though wondering how good a dinner they'd make.

She stared at her feet to avoid Algernon's penetrating eyes.

"We'll bring them back to Belesse," he told his men. But then he glanced around as though he'd just realized something was wrong. He settled his gaze on Baylen. "Where's your brother?"

"Brother?" Baylen said innocently.

Algernon folded his arms across his chest.

"Oh." Baylen gave the nervous grin again. "Leonard? You mean where's Leonard?"

Algernon watched Baylen, and Baylen watched Algernon.

"In serf Guillaume's pond," Deanna said. At least she didn't have to carry Leonard on her conscience anymore.

The wizard didn't point out that it was late for swimming, even though it must be five o'clock in the morning, if not later. The night seemed determined to last forever. He sighed. "Norman," he said, "why don't you take Baylen to Guillaume's holding? See if Leonard needs rescuing."

The young servant saluted sharply, all the while sucking in his cheeks to keep from laughing. Perhaps that should have made Deanna feel better about Baylen leaving her and Oliver alone with Algernon and all his armed guards. It didn't.

The wizard took off his helmet and squirmed out of the armor he'd worn to hide in the cauldron. Like Oliver, he was dressed in black. But while the dark against Oliver's fair skin made him look dramatic and interesting, it made Algernon look positively cadaverous. Her watch still hung around his neck by the gold chain she'd seen that evening. "Torrance, you make sure our young friend doesn't try anything foolhardy," he told the burly man who was guarding Oliver. "The rest of you can bring all this back to the castle." He ignored the groans of complaint and indicated for Deanna to follow Oliver and the man Torrance.

But things quickly turned nasty: Torrance took Oliver by the arm and Oliver twisted away from the touch. The guard roughly took hold of him again and Oliver looked ready to fight about it. "Oliver," she said.

Oliver narrowed his eyes.

He's not going to listen to me, Deanna thought.

However, when Torrance tugged on his arm once more, Oliver went with him quietly.

Deanna was aware that Algernon had taken in all this.

"Who are you?" he asked as they started toward the castle. "And what are you doing here?"

"That's for me to know and for you to find out," she said, estimating, after she'd already said it, that it made her sound about five years old.

"This . . . thing, which Baylen called a watch: What is it?"

"Never saw it before," Deanna said—so what if he knew it as a lie?

"The numbers change."

"Do they?"

"They count something. But they count strangely. They go to fifty-nine, then start all over again."

Sounded like seconds mode: the button must have gotten pressed while she tried to disentangle the watch from her sweater, sitting—all that while ago—on the side of the well in Chalon. She didn't say that; she said, "That is strange."

He grabbed her arm and swung her around to face him.

She scrunched her eyes closed to avoid his eyes.

"What's a Taiwan?" he fairly screamed, shaking her. "Who's this creature with the big ears and the long nose and the white gloves?"

"I don't know. Leave me alone."

She heard a scuffle from up the road and looked. Oliver was struggling with Torrance. The bigger man had him on his knees, his arms twisted up behind his back, but Oliver was still fighting to get back to her, to protect her. "It's all right," she called, thinking, *If Torrance hurts him, I'll . . .* She didn't know what she'd do, but she was determined that she'd make him pay somehow. "I'm all right, Oliver."

Oliver stopped struggling and Torrance hauled him to his feet. Algernon released Deanna, and Oliver let himself get yanked around, back toward the castle.

"What do the numbers count?" Algernon asked from between clenched teeth.

"Beats of your heart," Deanna said, spitting out the words as fast as she could think of them. "Each time your heart beats, the watch subtracts a day from your life. Take it off soon or you may well drop dead before breakfast."

She was angry enough to be careless. She let her eyes meet his. But he was angry also, angry and scared, in no mood to try mind control. He shoved her, hard enough that she had to take two quick steps, not hard enough to hurt, or to make her fall.

They walked the rest of the way in silence. The sky was definitely getting lighter. Castle Belesse loomed darkly ahead of them, looking for all the world like a fortified prison. The drawbridge was open, as it had been all the while she'd been here. Torches burned at that entry and at the entry to the main building. The courtyard was faintly illuminated by the torches along the inside of the encircling wall, but there were no lights showing in any of the windows. Except for a lone guard pacing along the top of the wall, no one seemed to be stirring at this early hour. *Seven o'clock?* she guessed. *Seven-thirty?* Normally she got up at seven-thirty. She'd never before been the whole night without going to bed. The cooking staff would be awake and about, but busy in the kitchen. No one would know where Algernon was taking them. No one would know he had taken them. *People disappear,* Leonard had told her.

She must have unintentionally balked, or Algernon expected her to try to escape, for he took firm hold of her arm. In the silent dawn their footsteps clattered noisily on the drawbridge. Noisily enough to wake castle sleepers? She doubted it. Should she scream? Should she assume Sir Henri would defend her against his own brother?

"To the tower, sir?" Torrance asked.

"Stable."

So he had something planned for them. Something so terrible he didn't dare do it here at the castle where normal (more or less) people could find out about it. She remembered Baylen summoning him to the stable to deal with a horse with a broken leg. She stiffened, refusing to walk. If she screamed and nobody came, still that wouldn't make their situation any worse. It could only help. Perhaps the wizard sensed the scream building in her throat, for he clapped his hand over her mouth. "Come on," he muttered between clenched teeth. She let herself drop so that he had to support her weight. His free hand circled her waist and he started dragging her across the courtyard, away from the entry hall, away from civilized behavior. "I'm not going to hurt you."

Sure he wasn't.

She tried to bite his hand, but it was large, and firmly centered over her mouth, and she couldn't get to it. Already they were away from the main entry, halfway to the stables. Her heels had left tracks in the packed earth of the courtyard. Would anyone notice and wonder? She could smell the animal pens: the goats, the pigs, the horses.

"Move," Algernon snarled at a clutch of half-grown chickens too intent on pecking at something in the dirt to get out of his way.

Oliver must have thought he was snapping at her, or he heard her muffled cries for help. In any case, he whirled around, and Algernon hissed into her ear, "Stop being stupid." And Torrance, who appeared to be the kind of man who didn't mind hurting people, drew his sword. It left its sheath with a sibilant whisper reminiscent of Aunt Emilienne sharpening her kitchen knives. The slitty-eyed expression Oliver wore reminded Deanna that he was used to claws and teeth: he was probably imagining himself going for Torrance's throat. *Don't fight him,* Deanna wanted to warn him, but Algernon's hand still covered her mouth.

Her watch intervened.

Or, rather, the musical alarm did.

"Dah-da dah-da dah-da dah . . ." It gave its tinny rendition of the opening notes from the "Mickey Mouse March."

Two bars into it and Algernon had let go of her and ripped the chain from his neck and was holding the watch away from himself at arm's length.

Drop it, Deanna wished at him.

He looked at it in horror, his hand tight on the chain.

Drop it, drop it.

The music stopped, its message complete. (Seven-thirty, time to get up.) He looked from the watch to Deanna. He wasn't going to drop it. He wasn't going to stampede in helpless panic.

But the pigs were.

Behind him, the pigkeeper's charges had roused themselves from dead-asleep to oinking, snorting pandemonium.

"Down, Squeakers. Back off, Patch," the little pigman cried. He'd been asleep on a pallet in one corner of the pen, and he rubbed his eyes with one hand, tried to restrain the pigs with the other. They continued to squeal and hurl themselves against the gate and the sides of the pen. "Charlemagne, you stop that right now."

Torrance, looking at the swirl of pigs open-mouthed, had let his sword arm drop. He and Oliver backed away from the gate, which rattled loosely in its rawhide bindings. Deanna and Algernon backed away from the side of the pen, which looked considerably less secure than it had five seconds ago.

"Patch! I'll stew you for dinner for sure 'less you get away from there!" No sooner said than the old man looked up and saw Deanna. Saw Algernon, with one hand still gripping her arm, the other holding out her watch. She saw something go on behind those eyes—she didn't know what. "Yey!" he called, giving the nearest pig a smack on the rump with the flat of his palm. "Walk! Walk time." And with that he flipped the rawhide thong that held the gate closed. "Yey, pigs! Walk!" A diversion!

The pigs headed for the courtyard.

Or, to be more precise, the pigs headed for Deanna and Algernon, who were standing between them and the courtyard.

The pigman put his hand next to his mouth and gave a cry that was half yodel, half yell. "Yah-yah-yah-yah! Snowy! Blacky!" One pen over, between them and the courtyard, a pair of young goats jumped their fence.

"Hey!" their keeper yelled at the pigman. "Don't do that." Too late.

The goats were headed for the pigman.

Or, to be more precise, the goats were headed for Deanna and Algernon, who were standing between them and the pigman.

Deanna scrambled up onto the railing of the pigpen. Algernon was half a step behind her.

"Whoa, Charlemagne! Back, boy." The pigman stopped the biggest of the pigs from getting past them. He headed it off toward where Algernon was perched on the fence. Other pigs got confused and started milling about, bumping into each other and into the side of the pen.

Deanna felt the boards rattle under her. Algernon had his knees pulled up to his chin.

Meanwhile the boy who tended the goats had

opened the gate to his pen in order to lead the two escaped goats back in. Instead the others got out.

"Bah! Bah!" they bleated, heading straight for the confusion. "Oink! Oink!" the pigs snorted. The dust they raised swirled thickly. The goats were the worst. They butted, some gently, some not so gently, against the pigs and the pen and the other goats. One began to nibble at Algernon's left sleeve while he had his attention on holding the watch away from another on his right side. As soon as he got distracted by noticing what was happening to his shirt, Deanna thought, she was going to grab the watch and run.

Servants poured out of the castle and the outbuildings. They shouted questions, yelled advice, and chased after the animals, riling more than they captured. Geese honked and beat their wings. Between them and the chickens, there was a snowstorm of feathers in the air. A rooster settled itself on the rail beside Algernon and began to crow.

Torrance had been elbowed away from Oliver, back to the fringe of the group. Good. Deanna decided to add to the confusion. She covered her ears against the din and began to scream as loudly as she could.

She could see the pigman jumping up and down, flapping his arms. Judging from the faces he made, he was also hooting, but she couldn't hear him over the other noises.

Oliver waded through the animals and people to get to her side. She uncovered her ears and was about to warn him that Torrance was making his way through the crowd, his sword still drawn, but Oliver wasn't even looking at her. His attention was straight on Algernon.

For his part, the wizard had finally noticed that half his left sleeve was eaten away. He was looking at that, so he didn't even glance up at Oliver's approach. But if Oliver had looked eager to get at Torrance's throat, Deanna thought he was going to kill Algernon.

He gave a shove that sent the wizard flipping backward into the pig yard, then hurdled the fence and jumped on top of the older man as he lay stunned, flat on his back in the muck. The watch had gone flying through the air, hit the gatepost, and landed on the chaos side of the railing.

"Fight! Fight!" various voices announced, a few sounding downright pleased about it.

Deanna took her eyes off the watch long enough to make sure Oliver was in control of the struggle inside the pigpen, then lunged after it. She dived between several sets of legs, human and not, and saw it kicked out of her range just as she was about to grasp it.

There. She crawled forward, almost got a finger stepped on, then cupped her hand over it. *Got you, got you, got you.* She sent a mental thank-you to the pigman.

A foot came down on the trailing chain Algernon had attached. Deanna pried at the foot and pushed against the leg. Nothing. "Excuse me," she said to the kneecap. Still the leg didn't move. Once again Deanna tried to wiggle her fingers under the boot. "Move, you medieval moron," she muttered. Still nothing. What kind of idiot was this? She took a second look at the boot. High-quality craftsmanship evident there. She moved her gaze slightly higher. The cloth of the pants was finely woven. Higher still, a brocade vest. Higher still to the face looking down at her with incredulous puzzlement . . .

She gulped.

"Hello, Sir Henri," she said.

16 / Explanations

Sir Henri leaned over and scooped up the watch. "Lady Deanna," he asked, "what are you doing?"

"Trying to rescue the world," Deanna mumbled. The situation hadn't merely taken another turn for the worse, it had just gotten hopeless. What now?

Sir Henri tapped his ear, indicating that he hadn't heard.

"Trying to rescue the world!" Deanna shouted. So what if he thought she was crazy? He'd never help her against his own brother. *People disappear,* Leonard had said. Despite all appearances, Sir Henri had to know, had to have been—if not a part of that—at the very least turning his back on the castle's darker goings on. Did she really think he'd consider her a special case, deserving of his intervention?

Sir Henri shook his head, and it took her a moment to realize that he wasn't answering her unspoken train of thought, but was simply showing that he still couldn't hear.

"Quiet!" he bellowed over the racket of squealing, squawking livestock and shouting, shoving humans. "Hold still."

Miraculously—she would never have guessed Sir Henri could command such authority—the humans in the crowd stilled. The animals, no longer pursued by whooping, arm-flailing servants, began to settle down. High-pitched squeals became grunts, the goats stopped butting, dust and feathers settled to the ground.

"You—" He pointed at someone behind Deanna. "—and you: break up that fracas. You, you, and you: round up the animals. The rest of you: don't try to help. Just stand perfectly still and don't make any noise. Let the animal keepers work around you. Lady Deanna." He helped her to her feet.

Even before she was standing straight, she looked for Oliver. He and the wizard Algernon were in the pigpen, held apart by two no-nonsense men. By their bulging muscles and sooty leather aprons, Deanna knew them to be the blacksmith and his assistant. The younger man, the assistant, had released the wizard but stood between him and Oliver, ready to keep them from getting at each other again. Algernon ignored him. He brushed off his clothes, his expression one of barely restrained fury. Oliver, on the other hand, seemed willing to take on the blacksmith despite the almost ludicrous difference in their sizes. But the huge man held him effortlessly, waiting for Sir Henri to tell him what to do next. Neither Oliver nor Algernon appeared to be seriously injured.

Then she took in the courtyard. It looked like the scene of a major pillow battle. The animals were being led back to their pens by the pigman, the goatboy, and the goosegirl, but feathers wafted through the air, stirred by their every move. The servants, who had been ordered not to move, were all facing her, watching her, waiting to see what she would do next.

Deanna closed her eyes and tried to pretend they weren't there. It didn't work.

"Now," said Sir Henri. "For shame."

Deanna peeked, and saw that Sir Henri was addressing Oliver and Algernon.

"Is this honorable? Is this sporting? I am deeply shocked by both of you. Surely this isn't the custom in Bretagne, sir."

Oliver, still struggling in the blacksmith's grip, caught sight of Deanna. For a moment their eyes met. He stopped trying to get loose. His anger seemed to dissolve all in a moment and he met Sir Henri's gaze levelly and coolly.

"And you, Algernon. At your age!" He gazed around the courtyard. "What is the meaning of all this? What's going on?"

That was a mistake. Everyone started at once.

"He's trying to kill us." Deanna pointed at Algernon.

"They're a danger to us." Algernon pointed at her.

"They're elves." Torrance pointed at her and Oliver.

The others wouldn't be outdone. The goatboy stuck his finger in the pigman's face. "He set my goats loose."

The pigman blamed it on the goosegirl. "She stepped on Patch's tail."

She wasn't paying attention. "Has anybody seen my goslings?" she asked.

Voices joined in from the crowd.

"Somebody picked my pocket."

"I didn't see anything."

"He started it."

"No, *he* did."

"No, she did."

Everybody seemed to have something to say, except Oliver, of course, who just stood watching her with those cold green eyes.

And then, from the back of the crowd, a peevish voice complained: "She stole my clothes."

That got everyone's attention.

Oh, no, Deanna thought.

Leonard made his way through the crowd. He was wearing what must have been clothing borrowed from serf Guillaume or one of the other holders between the pond and the castle: a burlap sack of a shirt and a pair of often-mended pants held up by a length of rope. He wore no shoes but had a narrow, moth-eaten blanket around his shoulders. "She—" He paused to give a great sneeze, and wiped his nose on the corner of the blanket. He pointed at Deanna. "She stole my clothes."

Deanna had to try twice before she got her voice to work. "I did not."

"Baylen told me all about it," Leonard told his father, and the whole courtyard of people. "She forced him to take my clothes."

"I forced Baylen?" Deanna cried. She spotted the older brother at the fringe of the crowd, wearing a sheepish grin. The cowardly little weasel.

Now Algernon hustled forward.

"Don't let him look in your eyes," she screamed at Sir Henri. Yesterday, when the wizard had stopped controlling her to try his spell on Oliver, she had seen that he could only affect one person at a time. But Sir Henri would be the worst one to be subject to Algernon's will. She protected her eyes with her hands.

"What?" Sir Henri asked, sounding no more befuddled than usual.

"These people are not what they seem," Algernon told his brother in a highly agitated voice. "They're not of this world."

"She stole my clothes."

"Leonard," the wizard said, "this is more important than your stupid clothes. They—"

"She stole . . . She . . . She . . . A-choo!"

"Has anyone seen the goslings?"

"Do you think she's the one who picked my pocket?"

"Henri, listen to me—"

"Maybe she stole your goslings, too."

Sir Henri's voice cut across all the others. "All right, that's enough!"

Slowly Deanna uncovered her eyes.

"That's enough," Sir Henri repeated, not quite a bellow this time. "We shall not have another public brawl. We shall discuss this in private, with decorum and reason. Algernon, Deanna, and Oliver, the four of us shall retire to my room and get to the bottom of this. Leonard, kindly change out of those ridiculous clothes and go blow your nose properly. Baylen, meet me in your room. Torrance, get these feathers cleaned up. And the rest of you can find something to do before I have to assign tasks."

That threat got the same reaction that it did whenever Deanna's teachers used it in school.

"Sir Henri—" Deanna said, fighting the stampede of people who scurried to exit the courtyard before they got noticed.

"My room," he said.

She sighed.

She turned and found Oliver still standing in the pigpen, the blacksmith gone. Almost everyone was gone already. The pig keeper was there, of course. He gave a shrug as though to say, *Well, I tried. But you keep messing up.*

She sighed again. "Come on, Oliver." She reached to give him a hand over the railing, although he probably didn't need it. He was watching her, she thought, with more hostility than usual. She was in no mood for his moods. "Let's go," she said testily, her patience gone, her nerves frazzled.

"You had it," he said softly, so that Sir Henri and Algernon wouldn't hear.

"Yes. For a moment. I let it get away." She didn't need his criticism. "I did my best." She wasn't used to people counting on her. She could grow to hate it very easily.

"You had it," Oliver repeated. "I felt you touch it."

"Oliver, would you get out of there?" She hadn't meant to yell, but she couldn't take much more of this. If he made her cry, here, where everybody could see, she'd never forgive him.

Oliver climbed over the railing, then stood there, just looking at her.

Algernon was watching their every move.

Sir Henri was yawning and scratching his head.

"You go first," Algernon told him, moving to place them between himself and his brother. "I'll guard the rear."

"Oh, don't be ridiculous." Sir Henri grabbed his arm and marched him toward the castle.

Deanna and Oliver followed. Up the stairs. Down the corridor. Around the corner. With Sir Henri's room in sight, she suddenly stopped and faced Oliver. Sir Henri and Algernon were still walking, Algernon looking over his shoulder to make sure they were still there, Sir Henri pulling him along. "What did you mean, you could feel it?" she whispered to Oliver.

He'd been watching her, she realized, still quietly, intently watching her. Instead of answering, he asked, "Why did you scream?"

"What?"

"Why did you scream? I thought he'd hurt you."

She remembered Oliver's face as he had gone after Algernon.

Algernon and Sir Henri had reached the door and were waiting for them. Close enough to see, not to hear.

"No. No, I wasn't hurt. I was just trying to add to

the confusion. I thought if things got hectic enough, I could maybe get to the watch."

He gave his head the upward tilt which he did instead of nodding.

It was her turn for a question. "What did you mean when you said you could feel me touch the watch?"

Finally he broke eye contact, the first time she had seen him do that. Instinctively, she lowered her gaze in response. Always before he either didn't even seem to notice her or he stared until she became disconcerted and turned away. He was learning the social amenities. Don't spit out the wine. Lie with a straight face. Glance away if you don't want people looking at you, especially if you have something to hide. He was learning—just in time to lose it all.

She looked up. Oliver was staring at the floor, his hands clenched by his sides. "When you touched the watch," he said softly, "you must have momentarily broken the chain of events that led to a change of history. For those few seconds, things were as though you had never dropped your watch into the well. The world reverted to what it had been before. I started to change back into a cat." He glanced up quickly to see her reaction.

She had never been sure how much of the situation he understood. She felt cold and drained. Somehow she had hoped . . . She had hoped . . . She didn't know what she had hoped. She only knew what she felt. "I see," she said, hardly any sound at all coming from her. This time it was she who broke eye contact.

Sir Henri cleared his throat loudly, and she welcomed the excuse to turn away from Oliver.

Sir Henri's room was cluttered with jousting prizes and tournament memorabilia. "Sit down," he said, then looked around at the mess. "Ahm . . . anywhere."

He sat on the corner of his bed and patted the spot next to him.

She waited for Algernon to sit on the window ledge to make sure he didn't hem her in, then took the place next to Sir Henri. Oliver sat on the edge of a chest strewn with brittle laurel wreaths and began to dust himself off.

"Now," Sir Henri started.

"They're not human," Algernon interrupted. "At least the boy's not."

Oliver, still fastidiously trying to get the dust out of his clothes, glanced up sharply.

Sir Henri gave the wizard a dirty look. "Now," he repeated to Deanna in a tone that said *No more interruptions,* "Torrance said you were elves. Surely—"

"Torrance is an idiot," Algernon said.

Sir Henri sighed.

"What that is—" Algernon indicated Deanna's watch, which Sir Henri still held. "—I have no way of telling. It's like nothing I've ever seen. The boy's sword is elfinwork. That much was immediately obvious: the craftsmanship, the metal itself—made of some substance I've never seen before, definitely not iron. But Torrance has an iron sword and it had no discernible effect on him. Everyone knows elves can't stand the feel of iron."

Incredibly, Oliver wasn't even paying attention. He was running his fingers through his hair, trying to remove the dirt from the courtyard brawl.

Sir Henri said, "And yet you say—"

"And yet I say he isn't human. Henri, I tried the mind-control spell and it didn't work on him."

That was it, Deanna thought. Her last hope had been that Sir Henri was somehow unfamiliar with what was going on, that he would be shocked to learn of Algernon's ways. Yet here was Algernon blithely saying *I tried the mind-control spell* just as easy as someone would say *I tried the new video game at the mall.*

"You know I don't like you using your mind-control spell on castle guests," Sir Henri said.

Well, there was an eloquent rebuttal. That certainly put Algernon in his place.

But, incredibly, Algernon did look disconcerted by it. "Henri, I had to. You don't understand how dangerous these two are."

Deanna looked to Oliver for support, but he was still preoccupied with getting all the grime off himself. He was wiping his hands on his pants but obviously wasn't satisfied. Any moment now, she thought, he would start licking them clean, and how would she ever explain that?

She didn't have to. From the room next door came a scream.

In that first frozen moment Deanna tried to relate the scream to what was going on with her and Oliver and the watch in this room, and couldn't. Then the voice began yelling, "Help me! Do something!"

In the next moment they were all on their feet. Sir Henri got to the door first and flung it open hard enough that it slammed into the wall and bounced back in the way of Deanna behind him. It only delayed them a second and they were all right behind Sir Henri as he raced down the hall and burst into the other room.

The first thing Deanna saw was Leonard, the ratty peasant's blanket still around him. He was in front of a chair, as though he had just stood up, his feet in a bucket of steaming water. But certainly it hadn't been Leonard who had screamed; Deanna was sure the voice had belonged to a woman.

And there was a woman in the room, a servant girl, who was standing by the fireplace, which she had apparently lit to get Leonard dry and warm. Even as Deanna registered that thought, Algernon shoved her out of his way so that she would have fallen if Oliver hadn't been behind her to hold her up. Algernon ran to the servant girl, grabbed her by the shoulders, and threw her down on the floor.

It was only then that Deanna realized how smoky the room was, and how the smoke smelled funny: like the time cousin Sid had dropped a cigarette ash onto Aunt Verna's expensive new sweater. Like burning wool.

She clutched at Oliver's arm, still around her.

The servant girl screamed again as Algernon rolled her on the floor and tried to beat away the flames that were eating away at the skirt of her long gown. But it wasn't only her gown that was ablaze. She must have accidentally dragged her skirt through the fire, then tried to brush the burning cinders away: the floor-to-ceiling tapestry on the nearby wall had ignited also.

Sir Henri took a step forward, then seemed to remember that his hands weren't free. "Here," he said, shoving the Mickey Mouse watch at Deanna. He strode forward and yanked the tapestry off the wall. Dust and burning bits of fabric flew into the air, then wafted down on air currents.

Deanna's eyes darted back and forth as she tried to keep track of all the leaf-thin glowing fragments, to make sure they didn't start their own fires.

The servant girl continued to scream. She was so frightened she was fighting Algernon's attempts to beat out the flames with his hands.

"Throw the rug on her!" Deanna cried, meaning the fur floor covering. Her hand closed convulsively, praying that Algernon could smother the flames before they ate through the thick woolen clothes to the girl's legs. She became aware of the watch biting into her palm.

Their problem, a tiny inner voice told her. *Take the watch and run.*

But Sir Henri, stomping on the burning tapestry, didn't seem to be doing much good; and if the fire got out of control, the whole castle could go. And no fire trucks for at least several hundred more years.

Your life's in danger, too, the voice said.

Oliver was still holding her, watching her, waiting for her. With no pockets in her gown, she shoved the watch down the front of her dress and ignored the little voice which called her an idiot. "What we need is water," she said.

With a tilt of his head, Oliver indicated Leonard, who was still standing in the water bucket.

"Leonard, get out of there," Deanna said.

If Leonard heard, he gave no indication. He just stood still, his eyes wide in horror.

Oliver gave him a push, so that he fell backward into his chair, then pulled the bucket out from under Leonard's feet. Oliver struggled, but managed to lift the heavy bucket. "Now what?"

Algernon had put out the fire in the servant's skirt, so she pointed to the tapestry and said, "Throw the water over there."

Oliver hesitated. "Sir Henri's in the way."

"Just throw it."

He looked at her in stunned disbelief. "It's water," he said.

"Oliver, throw it!" she screamed.

Oliver threw it.

The water hit Sir Henri, but it hit the tapestry too. There was a sizzling, then a smell of wet—as well as burned—wool, then Sir Henri and Algernon stamped out the last of the flames where the water had missed.

"Fast thinking," Sir Henri said to Deanna and Oliver. "Good work." He turned to the servant girl. "Are you all right, my dear?" he asked as water dripped down his collar.

She nodded, wiping her sooty hand across her cheek.

"Are you sure? You're unharmed?" Sir Henri seemed torn between modesty and the desire to check the girl's legs for himself. He helped her to her feet and brushed ineffectively at her scorched dress.

The girl forced a smile and curtsied. "I'm so sorry—" she started.

"Nonsense, nonsense," Sir Henri said. "The important thing is that everybody's all right. Leonard?"

"Ah . . ." Leonard said, still looking somewhat dazed.

"And you're not burned at all?" Henri asked the girl again.

She shook her head and began to blush at all the attention.

"Well then, no harm done. Why don't you get somebody from the kitchen to clean this up, and you take the rest of the day off. You've had a nasty scare."

"Thank you, sir." The girl dipped into another curtsy, and yet another for Algernon, then she scurried away.

"Leonard, why don't you go to your brother's room for now?"

"Ahh . . ." Leonard said.

Sir Henri took him by the arm and led him across the hall, both leaving a wet trail behind.

Deanna stole a look at Algernon, who had not acted as she would have anticipated, and saw that he was watching her. Oliver was, too. She stared at her feet.

Sir Henri came back across the hall. "We need to finish talking," he said, and led them back to his room. He took an extra blanket off the bed and wrapped it around himself. "Now," he said. "What were we talking about?"

Algernon wouldn't stop looking at Deanna. "We were talking about Lady Deanna's watch."

"That's right." Sir Henri scratched his head. "Now where did I put that?"

Deanna considered saying *Gee, I don't know,* but

with her luck Algernon had seen. "Excuse me." She turned away and fished the watch out from her dress. She held on to it tightly.

"And," said Algernon, "we were talking about dangerous people."

"Dangerous?" That was the last straw. *"Dangerous?* You're the one who's dangerous. Affecting people's minds. Making people disappear. And what is it that lives in your room, Algernon? Explain that." But even while Deanna challenged him, she remembered how he had dashed to help the servant girl, how he had risked getting hurt for someone else.

"You can make people disappear?" Sir Henri asked in surprise. "You never told me that."

"I can't," Algernon said. "I never did."

He seemed so sincere when he said it, so genuinely baffled. "Leonard said so," Deanna persisted, but less sure of herself now.

"Leonard said people disappear?" Sir Henri mused. He snapped his fingers. "I'll wager he meant those elves last summer." He turned to Algernon. "Remember that tall, green-haired lad the goosegirl was swooning over all that while? And how angry she got that you sent him away?" He turned to Deanna. "Algernon didn't make them *disappear,* my dear. He just forced them to go back into the forest." Then, as though guessing her thought, he said: "*We* forced them into the forest. This is no place for elves, Lady Deanna. Their ways are strange and often incompatible with ours. They work for good, but their good isn't necessarily our good. They do things—and we can't begin to guess why."

Like leaving plant messages, Deanna thought. *Like giving me only enough information to confuse me.*

Sir Henri was still talking. "But Algernon does them no harm. He does no one harm. He's a healer. Why, just yesterday he healed a horse with a broken leg."

Deanna felt like a total fool.

"He works to protect us, the castle. That's all. I'm disheartened that you could have ever thought otherwise."

She examined his face. Perhaps Algernon was making him say this. But his eyes looked perfectly clear and alert. Or at least as clear and alert as they ever did. And the way the wizard had acted in Leonard's room . . .

"What about your room?" she asked. "There's something in there—"

"There are many things in there," Sir Henri said. "But Algernon has made them invisible to protect them from the servants, who have a tendency to go where they've been told not to. Let's see . . . He has owls, a monkey, several snakes. Oh, and then there's the slime monster. He's ugly as anything but very affectionate."

"Chemical experiments," Algernon added. "Not to mention the basilisk. Good thing for you that you didn't see him: a look into his eyes kills." He glared at her. "And what of you? Lying and sneaking around." He paused, then suddenly sat back and regarded her quizzically. "Until just now," he admitted. "You did help with the fire. Why didn't you leave when you had the chance? Why didn't you take your watch and flee back to . . . Bretagne?"

Wrong: she had been wrong about everything. She had seen only what she had expected to see and had refused to let anything else sink in.

"I never said we were from Bretagne," Deanna said. "At least, not until you did, Sir Henri." She looked from him, to Algernon, to Oliver, back to Sir Henri. She wasn't clever enough to be a convincing liar, she knew. When she had tried being devious, she had only gotten deeper into trouble. And even if she knew how to lie, she didn't know which lies would help and which would hurt even more. She sighed, took a deep breath, sighed again, inhaled again, and plunged into the truth. "I'm from a place called Greeley, Colorado. Oliver is from Chalon. You haven't heard of either place before because they don't exist yet, and they won't for another nine hundred years or so."

Sir Henri raised his eyebrows.

"You are elves," Algernon said.

"No. But they sent us here."

"Irresponsible time-meddlers."

That wasn't what she had expected him to say at all.

"Those elves have no sense. Time passes at a different rate in the forest, and there's one clearing in there that's . . . I don't know . . . like a seaport, leading to strange lands."

"A gateway," Deanna said. "A temporal loophole."

"Yes, exactly." For a moment he seemed pleased to be supplied with the exact words for which he had been searching, but then he frowned as though at further proof that she was in league with the elves. "You can't go around playing with time," he scolded her.

"One of these days, you're going to slip, you're going to make a mistake, and the world may never recover. When are you people going to learn responsibility?"

"I am *not* an elf," she said. If he started in on her the way the fair folk had done, she was going to throw something. "I am not an elf. I am not a friend of the elves. I am not working for the elves." He was listening—they were all listening—and she made a conscious effort to control her voice. "Something from my time—accidentally—fell through to your time. It was my fault. I didn't mean to do it—I didn't even know I was doing it. But I did it, and the elves won't let me return home until I get it back, because somehow it caused just what you said: a mistake from which the world—my world—never recovered."

"This . . . watch?" Algernon took the watch from her hand, and she didn't even know whether to resist. "What manner of implement is this?" he asked.

"All it does is measure the passing of time. Of itself, it's harmless. I wasn't telling the truth when I said it could shorten lives. But somehow, by its very existence here and now, it's changing the nature of things to come. It's destroying my world as it should be. It doesn't belong here."

"And you assumed that I would be the one to misuse its power?" Algernon asked. His question started indignantly but finished sounding distressed.

"Someone does." For goodness' sakes: if not him, who? "Today."

"I've done nothing with it," Algernon protested.

She glanced at Oliver. If Algernon was telling the truth, shouldn't Oliver be feeling the change?

He was watching her every move, never saying a word.

"I've done nothing with it," the wizard repeated. Suddenly he bit his lip. "Except send word about it to the bishop."

"The bishop?" she echoed. She remembered the fair folk's warning that the watch would cause dissension in the Church, enough dissension to form a schism, to destroy feudalism before its time, to prevent the flowering of the Renaissance, to lead to a twentieth century in which she was never born.

She must have paled or looked faint, for Sir Henri took her arm. "Are you all right, my dear?"

"That might do it," she told Algernon. "I think that's it."

"The bishop's not an evil man," the wizard said.

"It makes no difference. I know because, you see, the fair folk put a spell on Oliver so he could help me. When we got the watch away from you, I touched it, and Oliver felt . . ."

"A shifting," Oliver explained, his expression daring anyone to ask what the spell was.

No one did.

Algernon sighed. "I'm sorry," he said. He held the watch up by its strap and let it dangle in the sunlight that came through the window, and for one last moment Deanna doubted him and thought, *Oh, no! What idea have I put into his head?*

But then he held the watch out to her. "If it's that important, you'd better take it back," he said.

17 / Good-byes

Deanna took the watch quickly, before Algernon could change his mind, and fastened it around her wrist: 9:26, according to Mickey.

The first thing she did was glance at Oliver to make sure he didn't turn back into a cat then and there.

He didn't.

But he shuddered, wincing as though in pain. In a moment he had recovered. *He'll be okay,* she thought. After all, he'd started out as a cat and that was the natural thing for him to be. It was just that she'd gotten used to him being a person. She swallowed hard. He was looking at her with those big green eyes, still something of pain in them. And possibly there was fear there, too. It was hard to say.

Algernon stood. "Now what we have to do is get you back to the elves' clearing—to that temporal hole of yours—before something else changes which you have to fix. That was," he added as she got to her feet, "where I was planning to take you all along."

"I'm sorry for what I assumed about you," Deanna

said, extending her hand in apology. "I'm new at all this and I've been making one mistake after—" He kissed her hand and she felt her face grow warm. She'd never get used to that.

Oliver stood abruptly. Starting for the door, he walked between them, forcing the wizard to release her hand.

"Well, I'm glad that had a happy ending," Sir Henri said. "You find what you came for, everyone ends up friends, Baylen and I get to go to the tournament—"

He was interrupted by a knock on the door. His steward, Ransom, stuck his head in. "The bishop's here," he announced, "waiting in the Hall."

Algernon exhaled loudly.

Oh no. Why did things here never stay simple for more than two seconds at a time?

"I've got to get back by midday," she told them.

Sir Henri said to Algernon, "He's going to need a proper welcome from both of us, or he'll want to know why."

"I'll delay him a bit," Algernon offered. "You get one of the boys to take Deanna and Oliver to the forest."

"Baylen," Deanna said quickly. Weasel that he was, he was safer than Leonard.

"Makes no difference," Algernon said. (Ha! Not for him!)

"My sword," Oliver reminded him. "My dagger."

Algernon groaned. "They'll have been brought to the storeroom. The guard will never let you pass."

"Here, take this." Sir Henri pulled a signet ring from his finger. "Give it to the guard on duty," he told

Oliver, "and he'll return your weapons. Deanna, you go to the stable and tell the lad there to prepare horses for you, Oliver, and Baylen." He kissed her hand.

She stood on tiptoe to kiss his cheek. "Thank you for all your help."

"Well—" He looked as embarrassed as she had felt. "Things will certainly seem quiet without you. We'll all miss you both." He clapped Oliver on the shoulder. "Good luck to the two of you." He swept out of the room with his brother. "I wonder if the bishop is going to Wharton's tourney?" she heard him say to Algernon. And then they were gone.

And she was alone with Oliver.

"Are you all right?" she asked.

He was leaning against the doorway, looking as sick as last night when he'd eaten . . . whatever it was that he'd eaten. "It's starting," he said, though no change was evident.

"Good," she said. Then, reading reproach in his eyes, she tried to explain: "I mean, that shows Algernon can be trusted. That things are going . . ." Her voice got softer, all by itself. ". . . the way they should be."

He turned and left without a word.

Deanna wiped her sweaty palms on her dress. *Irresponsible,* Algernon had called the fair folk. He didn't know the half of it. Darn them. She gave a great sniff. Hay fever starting in early. Just what she needed.

She took one step into the corridor and ran into the tall, skinny goosegirl.

"Oh, miss," the girl said, "Lady Marguerite's been asking up and down for you."

Deanna covered the watch with her right hand, aware of the minutes passing by. "Tell her good-bye for me, will you? My quest—"

The girl took hold of her arm as she tried to ease by. "Oh, please, miss! She's been so upset since last night. She thought you'd left without telling her. Then when I told her the two of you were in the courtyard and that you'd gone to Sir Henri's room, she sent me to get you. Please. Your young man, he wouldn't stop at all. The lady, she'll be heartbroken if I have to tell her that."

Deanna sighed and restrained herself from sneaking a peek at her watch. After all, Oliver had to go all the way to the storeroom to get back his sword and knife, and Sir Henri had to explain the situation to Baylen. Surely she had a minute or two to spare. Algernon could handle the bishop at least that long. "All right," she said.

The goosegirl knocked on Lady Marguerite's door and Deanna walked in.

The room was just barely lit and Lady Marguerite was lying on her bed, the same as the first time Deanna had been here. But not exactly the same. Lady Marguerite had on her floppy sun hat and she stood when she saw Deanna. It was only then that Deanna noticed she was dressed entirely in her outdoor gear: high-necked, long-sleeved gown, gloves. She even wore riding boots. "Deanna, dear," she said, "I'm so relieved, I was so afraid you'd gone."

"I wouldn't have left without saying good-bye," Deanna said. "Well, good-bye."

"I knew it: your quest calls you."

"Exactly. But I wanted to thank you. You've been so kind, so helpful."

"It was nothing. Here, do you think you can carry this —" She reached under her bed and pulled out a huge cloth satchel that looked rather like an overnight bag. "Or shall I call in some of the lads?"

"Ahmmm . . ." Deanna said.

Lady Marguerite picked up a second bag. "Personally, I think we can manage," she said.

"Ahmmm . . ." Deanna said.

"No need for us to call more attention to ourselves than we must."

"Ahmmm . . ." Deanna said.

"What is it?" Lady Marguerite asked. "Is something wrong?"

"I . . . I . . ." Deanna licked her lips, swallowed hard, and tried again. *"We?"*

"I beg your pardon?"

"We?"

"Yes, we. Us. Together. I'm coming along with you. On your quest. You, me, and Oliver. It'll be such fun."

"Lady Marguerite . . . I don't know what to say."

"Well then, say you'll carry the bag, and let's get going." She was beginning to sound impatient.

"What about your family?"

She shrugged. "It'll take them a fortnight to even notice I've gone."

"That's not true—"

"Deanna, please. I hate to say this, but really that's none of your business."

"But," Deanna said, "but—"

"Perhaps I should send for the lads after all."

"Lady Marguerite, please listen to me. You can't come with us."

"Well." Now she'd done it. Deanna could tell. "I really don't think that's your decision. At least not entirely. How about if we talk to young Oliver and see what he has to say?"

Deanna tried to calm her down again, to get the ice out of her voice. "You don't understand. We're not coming back here. Ever. Where we're going, it's a different world entirely."

"I do understand."

"But you don't understand about Oliver." She hadn't wanted to say that, to hurt Lady Marguerite's feelings, to sting her pride.

But then Lady Marguerite said, "Please don't get impertinent, Lady Deanna. I know you're from Bretagne and all, but—"

"Lady Marguerite, he's not what he seems."

"What he seems, my dear—"

"He's a cat."

"He's . . .?" Lady Marguerite laughed.

Deanna just stood there and watched.

Lady Marguerite's laughter petered off. "No, he's not," she said, very quietly.

"I'm sorry. But think about it. Think about what you've seen, what you've heard."

"No, he's not," Lady Marguerite repeated. But she sat heavily on the bed. Slowly, she untied her sun hat. She took it off and stared dully at it. "He's not." She looked up at Deanna.

"I'm sorry. He's under a spell. When we get back

home, he'll be a cat again. I should have told you before."

Lady Marguerite sniffled. "Well," she said. "My goodness."

Deanna sat next to her and put her arm around her shoulders. "I'm sure he's very fond of you, in his own way. He'll miss you, I'm certain. Here—" She stood up. "—let me get you a handkerchief."

"No, that's all right." Lady Marguerite gave another dainty sniffle and started to remove her gloves. "I'm not going to cry."

"Oh," said Deanna. "Well. Good."

"I never cry." She unlaced her boots. "It's bad for the complexion. Leaves one all damp and red and puffy. Causes wrinkles around the eyes. It's even worse for the face than laughing." She slipped her feet under the covers, without having taken off her dress. "I never laugh if I can help it," she said coolly. "And I never cry at all."

"I see," Deanna said.

"Have a good quest," Lady Marguerite said, not even looking at her, "You and What's-his-name."

"Thank you," Deanna said, backing away. "Goodbye."

Lady Marguerite removed two spoons from her night table and placed them over her eyes.

Deanna hesitated, but then closed the door quietly.

In the hallway, the goosegirl had gone, busy about whatever her morning tasks were. However, Deanna almost collided with another servant who was coming out of Baylen's room. That girl was carrying a water bucket. When Deanna glanced in the room, she saw Leonard sitting on the edge of his brother's bed, a fur skin wrapped around his shoulders, his feet once again in a bucket of steaming water. He looked up at that same moment and saw her.

"Leonard," she said.

"A-a-*choo!*" His sneeze shook his whole body, and water slopped out of the bucket onto the floor.

"Leonard—"

He snorted and turned his back to her.

She sighed. Well, perhaps that was all for the best.

She went down the stairs, around the back way to avoid the Great Hall, and into the courtyard. The pigman was there, walking the pigs.

She went up to him and said, "Thank you for your help."

"Well," he answered, "pigs, they like music. I whistle to them every day and they get used to things real fast, pigs do. They connect music with slops in the evening and walk time in the morning. They thought the wizard, there, was going to lead them around the courtyard, they did. And they was ready."

Algernon wouldn't have liked to hear that. "Yes, but you encouraged them. I hope you don't get into trouble."

The little man scuffed his feet in the dirt, bringing a flurry of feathers left over from the earlier scuffle and a scowl from the exhausted-looking Torrance who was still chasing after them. "Well, Sir Henri, he's a good man. You trust him, lady, he won't lead you far wrong."

She showed him the watch. “Algernon’s not so bad, either,” she said.

The pigman’s eyes widened, but then he gave a shrug as though to indicate he shouldn’t have been surprised. “Well, pigs always kind of took to him even before this morning. And pigs, they usually know.”

Deanna curtsied and he bowed, slapping his dusty hat against his dusty pants leg.

Coughing, she went to the stable to see if Baylen and Oliver were there yet.

18 / Going Home . . .

Oliver had made it there before her, but he hadn't gone in. He was half sitting, half crouching near the entrance, his arms around his knees, his back against the wall, which seemed made of little more than woven hay with a few wooden beams for support. If he was trying to make himself small and pathetic, he was doing a fine job of it. He didn't look up as she approached, and she stooped beside him.

"Are you all right?" she asked.

He nodded, never turning toward her.

"They getting the horses ready?" She was beginning to worry about the bishop and what could happen if they didn't get out of here fast enough. Too close to fail now.

He shrugged.

"Well, did you tell them?"

"No," he said.

"Why not?"

"Sir Henri told you to."

"Well then, I guess they aren't getting the horses

ready." She stood up, annoyed. Then she stooped down again. "Oliver." She put her hand on his arm. "What's—"

He jerked away from her touch and whipped around to glare at her. His eyes were full of pain and reproach.

And were slit-pupiled, like a cat's.

He must have seen from her face that the transformation was becoming visible. He bit off whatever he had been about to say and turned his back to her again.

"Oh, Oliver," she said, sitting in the dirt beside him. She put her arm around him. He didn't like it, she could tell by the way his back and shoulders tensed. "Oliver, I'm sorry." Was she going to spend the rest of her life apologizing for things that were beyond her control? "If there was anything I could do, you know I would."

Did he feel what she felt? Were his concerns and needs and hopes the same as hers? Or was she superimposing her wishes onto him, making a problem where none—or one totally alien to her perspective—existed?

He gave her a sidelong glance and said nothing.

"Oliver," she said, shaking him. "What is it?" And, oh how this hurt: "You're a cat."

"I know that." He rested his chin on his arms.

"Do you want to talk about it?"

"No, I don't want to talk about it." But then, very softly, he said, "I don't want to go back."

"To Chalon?" she asked.

"To being a cat."

She sighed. "I have no say in that, Oliver." Her heart was beating so hard it hurt. She didn't want to lose him, but she would in any case. She said: "If you stay here in this time, maybe you'll be all right. We'll explain to the fair folk—"

He turned away, angry.

Yeah, sure, the fair folk. Right. "Oliver—"

"Do you think I can go back after this? Be happy with what I was: rubbing against people's legs for attention, coughing up hairballs, eating mice in the barn? After this? Or won't I even remember? Will it be as though I never existed?"

That, in another form, was what the fair folk had predicted for her. She shook her head. "I don't know."

"I wish we'd never found it. I wish we could have stayed like this forever."

"But the fair folk said the world changed for the worse. And I would never get back home."

Before Oliver had a chance to answer, Baylen's voice carried over as he crossed the courtyard: "Deanna! Oliver!" He came, grinning all the way as though he had never tricked them and abandoned them and lied about them to get himself out of trouble. He stopped, standing close enough that his shadow fell across them. "Why the serious faces, you two?"

"Deanna was just explaining to me," Oliver said, getting to his feet but keeping his face tipped so that his eyes wouldn't show, "how her life is more important than mine."

"No," Deanna protested, scrambling to her feet, "that's not what I meant. Oliver!"

But he had already gone into the stable.

Baylen shrugged. "Strange," he said. "Very strange, that one."

Deanna bit off her answer, which was rude and wouldn't have helped the situation anyway, and followed Oliver.

The horse stable was large and well kept, which meant the smells of fresh straw and hay kept the more objectionable odors to a tolerable level. Stableboys were bustling about tending a half dozen richly caparisoned horses that had just been brought in: the mounts of the bishop and his retinue, Deanna realized, as she watched the boys remove brocade saddlecloths and harnesses hung with tiny silver bells.

The master of the stables had seen them come in. "More horses to be readied?" he asked Baylen, shouting over the confusion of feeding, watering, and currying.

Baylen held up three fingers.

"Justin!" the master called to a young boy who was sweeping out the stalls. "Three horses."

"Yes, sir."

"Ahmmm . . ." Deanna said.

"You don't ride?" Baylen guessed.

"No, I don't."

"Justin!" he called. "Two horses."

"Yes, sir."

"Oliver doesn't ride either," she pointed out.

"Of course he does," Baylen said. "Father taught him yesterday. He learned in no time."

Oliver learned a lot of things in no time, she thought.

"Still, it'd probably be best if you rode with me rather than with him," Baylen said, "since I do have a bit more experience." He grinned.

Oliver was busy ignoring them, so she nodded. It made sense.

The stableboy, looking hardly big enough to manage, got two of the horses harnessed and ready.

Baylen stuck his head out the door. "All clear," he announced. He swung onto his horse and held a hand down to her.

The animal looked a lot bigger than she'd imagined from seeing them on TV or grazing in far-off fields. It had large yellow teeth, and it snorted at her, watching her warily out of the corner of its eye, which did nothing for her confidence. The stableboy came up behind to help her on.

"Put your foot here," Baylen told her. "No, this way. Give me your hand. Don't lean that way. No. Deanna. Wait. This way. Keep your foot straight."

The stableboy, who had managed to lug around those huge saddles without any trouble, tried to lift her by the waist and shove her up the side of the horse, while Baylen grabbed her under her arms and tried to haul her up. *Nobody* touched Deanna under her arms. Even the thought of it was enough to tickle, to make her squirm. *The Lone Ranger never got on Silver like this,* she thought, aware that her rear end was sticking up in the air while her face pressed against the horse's scratchy neck. "There." Baylen gave a great heave and got her up in front of him and facing in the right direction, but sitting sidesaddle.

"I'm going to fall."

"You're not going to fall."

"I'm going to fall." She clutched at his arm.

"You're not going to fall. Here, lean against me."

She did, which made her feel slightly more secure. Just slightly.

"Relax, I've never lost a lady yet."

How reassuring.

Oliver had mounted already and was waiting patiently. Occasionally Deanna would catch a glimpse of his face, his eyes, and there was still pain there. She hated to see him go through this.

Baylen moved their horse to the stable door. "All cl— Oh-oh."

A tall man had just come out of the castle's front entry.

"The bishop?" she whispered, noting his fine clothes and the gleam of a huge gold cross hanging halfway down his chest.

Baylen nodded.

Algernon and Sir Henri followed close on the cleric's heels. One of them said something which made him turn away from the stable.

"We'll take it nice and slow and easy," Baylen said, urging the horse out into the courtyard and toward the front gate. Oliver's horse followed. Just three boring people out for a morning ride, their demeanor was meant to proclaim.

Sir Henri was pointing out some feature of the castle's roof to the bishop so that his back remained to them.

Their horses' hooves clattered on the wooden drawbridge, then thumped on the grass on the other side of the moat. Deanna didn't look back lest she draw attention to them by appearing anxious. Baylen checked over his shoulder as though to make sure Oliver was keeping up. "The bishop doesn't seem interested in us," he announced.

Deanna let out the breath she had been holding and glanced at the watch. 10:43. Had the fair folk been speaking literally when they'd said midday?

Baylen dug his heels into their horse's sides, and the animal leapt forward.

"Don't do that," she yelled at him, scrambling for a better hold. She was going to bounce right off, she knew it. Whoever had invented horseback riding as a mode of transportation had to have been a maniac. She flung her arms around Baylen's neck, because he seemed like the only steady thing in the world. The ground underneath her feet sped by dizzyingly and the wind whipped her hair against her face. The beating of her heart and the horse's hooves seemed to be keeping time. "I'm going to fall off," she yelled to be heard over the sound of both.

"You're not going to fall off," Baylen assured her once again and urged the horse on even faster.

Deanna peered around him sure that Oliver would never be able to keep up. What was Baylen doing, *trying* to lose him? But Oliver was staying with them nicely. She closed her eyes to protect them from the stinging tendrils of hair, and to protect her stomach from the sight of the lurching countryside.

Eventually—only about as long as ten or twenty trips up, down, and around on Space Mountain at Disneyland—she realized that they had slowed, and that the sun wasn't beating down so fiercely on her head. She opened her eyes gingerly, ready to shut them at the slightest hint of tipping landscape. But as she did so, Baylen pulled the horse in even slower, into what was probably called a trot. There were trees all around. They had entered the forest.

She craned to look around Baylen. Oliver had managed to stay with them. Now, if she could just refrain from throwing up, she'd be all set.

The clearing where she'd first met Baylen and his family was just inside the forest; they'd be there any second now. She tried to do some mental calculating to see how long it would take after that. She and Oliver had walked . . . what? about an hour between the fair folk's clearing and the one where the joust had taken place. Figure about a mile every fifteen or twenty minutes, that made approximately three or four miles. Okay, now how fast were the horses traveling?

She couldn't concentrate. First, there was the ever-present fear that she would yet bounce right off and land on her face in the underbrush. But also, now that she was thinking about that first day, she was remembering her first conversation with Baylen, and how unenthusiastically he had reacted to her request for help. What a coincidence that now he was helping her. Unexpectedly, Algernon's voice came back to her. Algernon's voice said: *I don't believe in coincidence, do you?*

She'd been holding on around Baylen's neck, but now she let go. Instead she clutched the saddle for support.

They broke through the trees into the first clearing.

Two men were there, waiting on horseback. One was Baylen's squire, Vachel, the other someone whose face was vaguely familiar from the castle. That should have meant that they were friendly, that Deanna had nothing to worry about.

Should have.

It took all her courage to release the saddle and to let herself slide down under Baylen's arm and off the horse. The thing was still moving, and she had a perfectly vivid picture of catching her foot and getting dragged under and trampled, something along the lines of the chariot scene in *Ben Hur*. None of that happened, of course. Sitting sidesaddle, she was facing off to the left anyway, and she started walking as soon as her feet touched the ground. The horse kept going, and Baylen was too surprised to react for at least a couple seconds.

"Oliver," she called, having visions of him spurring his mount to a gallop, swooping down on her, lifting her up onto his saddle, and riding off into the sunset with her.

None of that happened, either. Oliver was a quick learner, but apparently swooping was not one of the things that had come up in his lessons with Sir Henri.

Baylen wheeled his horse around and placed himself between Oliver and Deanna. "Oh, Deanna," he said innocently, as though he could think she had fallen off, "I'm so sorry. Are you all right?"

She backed away from him. "What are they doing here?" she asked.

"Them?" Baylen glanced at the men who were

slowly but steadily approaching. "I don't know. They must have decided to go out for a ride and happened to have chosen the same path we did."

Deanna remembered the stable master commenting on the number of horses Baylen was having readied that morning. "I see." She took another step back.

The two men had positioned themselves, one on either side of Oliver. Nothing openly hostile, but ready.

Oliver's strange slitted eyes flicked from them to her.

Baylen sighed. "Somebody get her back up on the horse, would you?" he snapped.

19 / ... Going Home ...

Rachel, the squire, dismounted and helped Deanna get back on Baylen's horse. It was a lot easier the second time, except that at the last moment Baylen swung her around so that she was straddling the horse. This was much more comfortable. But it was going to make getting off quickly just about impossible. He was scrunching her hat, which was still tied around her neck but had slipped down her back like a cowboy's hat.

"What are you doing, Baylen?" she demanded.

"Lady Deanna," he said, putting his hands on the reins, which meant around her also, "working with you on your quest these past several hours, I have come to a great appreciation of and admiration for your beauty and your spirit." He started the horse moving again, at a slow walk. Oliver rode behind, with the two men from Castle Belesse in the rear. "I have decided that I cannot survive bereft of your presence."

Could he possibly be serious? "You can't come with us," she said, incredulous that she'd had to say that twice this morning.

"That was never my intention."

"I can't stay."

He grinned.

A nasty suspicion settled in a cold, hard lump in her chest. She repeated: "I can't stay."

"Just for a little while."

The lump got colder and harder and, yes, lumpier. She hadn't believed for an instant—well, not for two instants—that she could sweep Baylen off his feet. But he could at least have tried for a convincing lie. *"Just for a little while,"* she echoed. "Just long enough for Leonard to hear about it."

"Well . . ." he said.

She followed Baylen's nasty reasoning. "If Leonard's going to look foolish for pursuing me if I just leave, he'll look much worse if I run off with you, is that it?"

"Well . . ." he said.

She sighed. It was her own fault, she thought, reflecting once again on that first meeting. She'd always been warned against talking to strangers. And Baylen was about as strange as you could get. His petty feud with Leonard was going to ruin everything. What now? *Help!* she could shout. *This man is not my father! This is not someone I know!* That certainly wasn't going to be a tremendous help in this situation. She glanced backward. Oliver was watching her. He wouldn't do anything without instructions. The two men from Castle Belesse were behind him, single file because the path at this point was so narrow. Not much he could do with them there anyway. Who else was a possibility? Sir Henri and the wizard Algernon were back at the castle detaining the bishop on her behalf. The fair folk had yet to provide overwhelming aid. She was on her own. She was used to depending on others, or on crossing her fingers and hoping for the best. But she was on her own. This time it was her or nobody.

How could she get off the horse? Or—and she liked this even better—how could she get Baylen off the horse?

She shifted her hold on the horse's neck so that her left arm was between the reins, where she could grab hold if need be. Then she waited until they came to a rough area on the forest path. It dipped where a big tree root had come up to the surface and weather had hollowed out a sizable nook in the road. Sturdy weeds grew around the tree, overflowing onto the path, making it even narrower.

She didn't dare look back to check on Oliver, lest Baylen get suspicious. But she estimated that his horse was about ten seconds behind theirs. She squeezed her legs tight around the horse as it stepped over the root. *One, two, three* . . . Was she counting too fast? . . . *four, five, six* . . . Was she counting too slow? . . . *seven, eight, nine* . . . Too fast and Oliver would still be behind the root when she went into action. Too slow and not only Oliver but Baylen's men would be past it. *Ten.*

Deanna leaned ever so slightly to the right as though looking down at their horse. "Why's he holding his leg funny like that?" she asked.

Baylen craned around her for a better look. "What?" he asked. "How?"

She shoved him with all her might.

Caught off balance, he didn't even have the chance to grab for support. He toppled from the horse, and the best he could accomplish was to twist his body so that he landed on his side rather than face first.

Deanna had been worried that she might have trouble getting the horse to move. No such luck. The horse, startled, bolted headlong down the path.

Deanna flattened herself along the horse's neck, holding on with arms and legs and willpower.

Behind her she heard men shouting. That sound faded almost immediately. Horse's hooves pounded, whether just hers or someone else's in pursuit she couldn't tell. She could smell the sweat on her horse's neck. He became slippery with it. Great drops of salty lather flew back into her face. Low-slung branches whipped by overhead. Tall bushes grazed her legs. The path twisted. Her rear end was slipping off to the right, and try as hard as she would, she couldn't seem to get herself properly centered. *You're falling. Let go of the reins,* she told herself. She'd fall for sure that way, but at least she wouldn't get dragged. She couldn't bring herself to do it.

But somebody was pulling up on the reins. Deanna had been concentrating so hard on holding on, she hadn't been aware of someone riding up next to her and grabbing the reins. Her face was pressed against the horse and she couldn't see more than the other rider's mount. Baylen, Oliver, or one of the others—she didn't care, so long as this wild ride ended.

Her horse snorted, tossed its head, slowed, stopped.

Drained of emotion as well as energy, Deanna raised her eyes. "Long time no see," she said.

"We *just* saw each other," Oliver told her.

"Never mind." She pulled herself up into a sitting position. "What's going on back there?"

"Baylen looks uninjured but annoyed. The two others were slowed by the condition of the road and by not wanting to trample him. Vachel's just behind me. Baylen stopped the other man to take his horse, so he's farther back. Do you want to ride with me?"

She nodded and he pulled the horses up next to each other. Deanna lifted her left leg up onto the saddle, then Oliver pulled her over onto his horse.

"Bring both horses," she said. "When the path divides, we'll go one way, send Baylen's horse the other. Let's hope Baylen and Vachel will separate."

Oliver gave Baylen's horse a slap on the rump, and it took off again. He tightened his arms around Deanna, and then they were off too. She felt considerably more secure with Oliver than she had with Baylen (and infinitely more secure than on her own), but still she couldn't imagine anyone doing this for pleasure. She checked the watch: it read 11:37.

The forest didn't look familiar. None of the fair folk's white linoleum with red polka dots, no flashing arrows. The path went up and down and twisted sharply among the treacherous trees. She wasn't even sure if they had been going in the right direction when they left the first clearing. "Fair folk, you better do something!" she shouted. The wind ripped the words away from her. No answer. She hadn't expected one.

"Up ahead," Oliver told her.

The path branched off. No telling which was the correct way. So when Baylen's horse chose left, they went right.

"Keep down," Oliver warned as a low branch came close to smacking her in the face.

That gave her an idea. "Oliver, are you a good climber?"

He didn't answer and she turned enough to see his face. He had on one of his long-suffering expressions.

"Right. Sorry. How about if we hide the horse, you climb one of these trees with a low branch, hold the branch back, then let it go when Baylen or Vachel comes by?"

Oliver didn't answer, but the next time they came to a suitable tree, he led the horse off the path and into the forest itself. He slid off and handed her the reins.

"Good luck," she said.

She could hear, from not too far behind, the pounding of hooves on the trail. One horse? Two? She wasn't experienced enough to tell.

Oliver said nothing. He climbed the tree faster than seemed humanly possible. Oh. Right. When was she going to catch on? In seconds, she had lost him among the branches and leaves.

There! She could make out a rider tearing down the path toward them. She didn't dare let herself be seen, so she couldn't move out and get a really good look. One man, though. If it was Baylen, that would mean that Vachel, who'd been in front, had taken the other route. If it was Vachel, that could mean that Baylen had taken the other route. Or it could mean that Baylen was just a little bit behind. Closer. Closer. The horse was bouncing so much she couldn't make out the face. Closer. She almost collapsed with relief. Baylen. They'd only have to deal with the one. Closer. He wasn't slowing down. He didn't see her. He was almost abreast of her. He passed her. He was at the tree. Passing under.

Oliver released the branch and it hit Baylen mid-chest, sweeping him off. The horse kept going, and Baylen just lay there on the road, flat on his back.

"Go," she told her horse.

It was nibbling on some grass and didn't even look up.

She gave the reins a tentative shake.

The horse snorted and shook its head as though at a persistent fly.

She nudged it gently with her heels and it finally left the grass alone and ambled back toward the path.

Oliver had jumped down from the tree, landing lightly, and he was stooped next to Baylen, who still had not moved. Deanna's relief began to shift to worry. "Is he all right?" she asked. If she had really hurt him, she'd never forgive herself.

Oliver turned Baylen's face. He had a nasty bump on the side of his head, and Oliver's hand came away bloody. It wasn't that serious, Deanna thought, but Oliver just stayed there, looking at his blood-smeared fingers.

"Oliver?"

He raised his fingers to his mouth.

"Oliver!"

He looked up sharply. The green, slit-pupiled eyes

looked at her coolly, appraisingly, like the eyes of the big cats in the Boulder Zoo, the big cats that they kept behind protective bars or ditches. *My, don't they look like big kittens,* someone would always say, until they let out a roar or lunged at the barriers. Deanna swallowed hard.

"He's knocked himself out," Oliver said, the same quiet, steady—human—voice as always. "He'll recover."

Deanna gave another swallow. "Then we'd best get out of here before he does," she said, her voice little more than a whisper.

"Best we do," Oliver said, watching her, gauging her reactions. He wiped the blood off on his pants leg, then took the horse's reins and swung up behind her.

In the moment that her attention was on Oliver remounting the horse, the road became covered with the familiar polka-dot pattern. An arrow flashed inches from Baylen's head, pointing the way they were already headed. "Fine timing," she muttered. She glanced at the watch: 11:52.

They rode in silence, 'til she could stand the silence no longer. But there was nothing to say, and they rode in silence some more.

She released the reins long enough to brush her hair off her face. Regardless of how long she *knew* Oliver had been riding, he seemed to have done it forever and she felt as much at ease with him as she would with anyone. That was true, she realized suddenly—despite everything—regarding more than just riding. She leaned against him for the reassurance of his being there.

They passed beneath a flashing neon archway. Trumpets blared. Fragrant rose petals wafted down from the highest branches. She recognized the pond edged by weeping willows, the wall of trees. Those miserable elves, she thought. Irresponsible, indeed. No sign of them. Just wait . . . just wait . . . Her eyes were beginning to get watery and she took hold of the reins again. She blinked several times. That wasn't going to help anything. She kept her head down lest Oliver see, and doing that noticed that his hands had changed. Still basically human, the fingers were shorter, the nails longer and curved along the sides. She started, despite herself, and stole a quick glance to see if there were any other visible changes. None so far. But Oliver caught her staring. He shifted position slightly, to tuck his fingers under, so they wouldn't show. "It's not fair," she insisted.

He shrugged.

"Oliver, take the horse. Go back. There's magic in this world. Algernon will help you. Sir Henri will take you in. Make a life for yourself here. The fair folk . . . the fair folk can't be trusted."

Oliver was shaking his head. "There's nothing for me here."

"Of course there is. Sir Henri likes you, Lady Marguerite likes— Oliver, I told her about you, but I don't think it'll make any difference. If you're there, I don't think she'll— Stop shaking your head. You know how fond she is of you and you are of her."

"Lady Marguerite?" he asked incredulously.

"And Algernon is ticked off at the elves as it is. I'm sure he'd be willing—"

"I'm not fond of Lady Marguerite."

"Come on, Oliver. It's all right. I could tell and I don't mind. You were with her every chance you got, smiling and chatting and—"

"You told me to."

"What?"

He pulled the horse to a stop beside the pond. Still the elves hadn't shown their sneaky little faces. "You told me to be polite, to be pleasant."

Deanna closed her eyes.

"You're the one I'm fond of. I came through the well for you, Deanna. I love *you.*"

Her heart seemed to stop. Her breath definitely did. She bit back her instinctive answer: *You're a cat, and you know nothing about it.* She chewed on her lip, trying to word out a better answer. But perhaps he had read the first one in her face. He looked away. What did Lady Marguerite or Sir Henri know about love? Or Leonard and Baylen? Or, at this point in their lives, her parents? Or, for that matter, what did she know about love? *He can't love me,* she thought. *He's a cat.* But then she thought: *Why not? He's a cat and I love him.*

She couldn't stand the thought of never seeing him again. She threw her arms around him, burying her face in his chest. "Oh, Oliver, I don't want to lose you."

He put his arms around her, slowly, gingerly, as though not sure what was expected of him.

She looked up and kissed him.

He smiled, sad and sweet. "No matter what you

do, I'm not going to change into a prince," he told her.

She couldn't help but smile back.

By her elbow a familiar voice sneered, "Well, you certainly took your time, human girl. Now, at last, things can go back to the way they were before."

"Listen," she said to the fair folk in the Hawaiian shorts (*Aloha* his shirt said, written in flowers and erupting volcanoes), "I've got the watch, but I—"

He reached over and shoved.

"Wait!" she screamed, tipping precariously. She was holding on to Oliver, but Oliver was falling too. Falling and falling and falling. She braced herself for a hard landing, but she hit the pond. *Can't be that deep,* she told herself at the first splash, *not right near the edge.* But the water closed over her head, singing gently to her. *Oliver!* she thought, but the water was cold and dark and she couldn't even tell which side was up and she couldn't find him and finally she wasn't aware of anything at all.

20 / ...Home

When the world came back into focus, the first thing Deanna was aware of was the grass tickling her stomach. She rolled over and sat up. She was wearing her jeans and rainbow sweater. Her entire back end was sore from the horse's jostling. No sign of the horse now. There was the well, smelling dry and old. Beyond that, she could just make out the orange tile roof of the Guyon farmhouse. Her clothes and hair were still wet enough to wring out.

Oliver she found sitting under some tall weeds, licking himself dry.

"Oh, Oliver," she said, scooping him up and holding him close. His black fur was thick and warm. She looked deep into his eyes and tried to figure out how much he knew, how much he remembered. No telling. Those deep green eyes had always given the impression that there was something going on behind them.

She leaned over the well. "Stupid elves!" she screamed. "Making shoes is all you're good for! Fairies! Pixies! Brownies!"

Far, far below, her voice reached the water, bounced off the mossy sides, and returned in a hollow echo.

"I hate you," she whispered.

She turned her back to them. But she couldn't return home, not now, not right away. She sat down heavily on the ground, her back against the rough wall of the well. Still holding Oliver close, she rocked back and forth. "Oh, Oliver," she said. "I'm sorry. I'm so sorry. I wish . . ." She started to cry. "I wish . . ."

Oliver stiffened, and behind her the well gave a definite gurgle.

Deanna sat up straighter. She gave a good hard sniff and rubbed her nose. "I wish," she said.

Oliver hissed.

"Shhh." She smoothed down his fur, which seemed to be all on end. *Things can go back to the way they were before,* the fair folk had said. She looked at her watch. The date hadn't changed from the first day. The time was about what it should have been had she never left. *Things can go back to the way they were before*. Before, she had started a wish and interrupted it by dropping her watch. Before, she had wasted the magic this well had to offer. Before, before. She stood up abruptly and Oliver jumped from her arms.

Absently, she wiped cat fur from herself.

I wish that Mom and Dad were back together again and that we'd all be happy again. That's what she had told herself she would wish if she ever got a second shot at it.

But you can't go wishing happiness on other people, she thought; you've got to make your own. People were going to be what they were going to be.

She looked down at Oliver, who looked up at her.

It'd never work. It was a stupid idea. He was a cat. People in tenth-century France had thought he was weird. How would he ever pass in twentieth-century America? Or twentieth-century France for that matter? He'd have no family, no personal history, no education. What could she say: *Look what followed me home, Mom. Can I keep him?* It was totally ridiculous. The problems were insurmountable.

She looked at the well.

She looked at Oliver.

She smiled.

Then again, she thought, what could she do but cross her fingers and hope for the best?

She leaned over the well and wished.

Vivian Vande Velde's previous book for Crown is *A Hidden Magic*. She lives in Rochester, New York, with her husband, daughter, and cat, which, as far as she knows, has always been a cat.